MW01232111

Not My Idea

A Gentleman of Misfortune, Volume 1

Bethany Swafford

Published by Lilac Petal Press, 2023.

NOT MY IDEA

First edition. June 26, 2023.

ISBN: 979-8885268417

Written by Bethany Swafford.

Table of Contents

Chapter One.. 1

Chapter Two.. 11

Chapter Three 21

Chapter Four 35

Chapter Five 45

Chapter Six 55

Chapter Seven 63

Chapter Eight... 75

Chapter Nine.. 91

Chapter Ten 103

Chapter Eleven..115

Chapter Twelve 127

Chapter Thirteen 137

Chapter Fourteen 149

Chapter Fifteen 161

Chapter Sixteen 177

Chapter Seventeen 189

Chapter Eighteen...201

Chapter Nineteen...211

Chapter Twenty 221

Epilogue..231

Lucas' story will continue in Best Laid Plans...................233

Chapter One..235

Acknowledgments..243

Also Available By Bethany Swafford...............................245

For my parents who taught me to love books

Chapter One

1814 *"Lucas, you must return home."*

Those words preyed on my mind as I rode through the county of my birth. That my father had not seen fit to explain *why* I needed to return home was more than a little annoying and I couldn't help but feel a sense of unease. I had never been summoned home in such an abrupt manner before and why had my father, who was usually direct about everything, sent such a brief, vague note?

I reined my mount to a halt on the hill that overlooked Bywood Hall, the home of my family for the past six generations. As I watched, the clouds parted to allow the sun's rays to illuminate the hall. The white limestone nearly glowed in the light and certainly added to the impressive stature of the house.

To my right, just a few miles away, was the Ramsey estate, Lamridge . That family had not been in the county as long as mine but my father and Mr. Ramsey were old school friends. Hardly a week passed in my childhood that we were not there or they were at the Hall. It was as familiar to me as my own home and the occupants as close as family.

A feeling of contentment, such as I hadn't felt in several years, settled around me. "Home," I said, patting the horse's neck. He tossed his head with impatience and I let out a laugh. "Yes, I understand. You want your feed. Let's go."

It only took the slightest nudge from my heels and we were off. In a matter of minutes, Bywood Hall loomed above us, and I took a moment to appreciate the stately structure that had been my childhood home. Even though I was now two and twenty, it made me feel tiny and insignificant—a state of mind my elder brother, George, would no doubt encourage me to indulge in more often.

I rode to the stables where I dismounted. A stable boy rushed to take charge of my mount. "He has had a long, hard ride, Cole," I informed the young man. "See he is rewarded and then returned to the Rose and Crown in the morning."

"Yes, Mister Lucas," the stable boy said, tugging the brim of his cap before leading the horse to the stable.

For a hired hack, he had been well trained and energetic, which was not usual to find. As it was, I was more than ready to have my own mount, Phaeton, to ride now that I was home. I could hardly wait for the opportunity to race across the countryside.

Taking a deep breath, I approached the front door, the feeling of apprehension returning once again. It didn't seem necessary to knock or ring the bell when it was all too easy to open the door myself. I shrugged my greatcoat off as I strode through the entry hall, the sound of my boots on the white marble floor echoing in the space.

A few moments later, Butler came hurrying forward. "Mister Lucas! Allow me to take your coat and hat, sir. I was not informed you were to return today and I did not hear the bell. My sincerest apologies."

"You didn't hear the bell because I did not ring it, Butler." I grinned at the middle-aged man who had served my family for as long as I could remember. How delighted I had been as a child that our butler's name was 'Butler'. "And I didn't send word ahead. I didn't think there would be any need."

"I will have Mrs. Stokes prepare your room for you right away," he swore, sending a look behind me. "Your valet will be arriving soon with your luggage?"

I waved a dismissive hand. "I found Waverly didn't suit me long ago, Butler." Waverly's dislike of travel had been reason enough for me to send him packing within days of our leaving Bywood Hall. "I believe he's doing rather well for himself in London, employed by some viscount...or was it a marquess? Anyway, he is much happier now."

Butler swung a horrified gaze back to me. "You don't mean to say you have no valet!" He straightened his shoulders as though he were going to take on some challenge. In reality, he was: me. "Mister Bywood and I will remedy this at once."

"I wish you would not."

And I was completely serious. I had managed well enough without the pretension of a valet for two years now and I could continue to do so. Shaking his head, Butler called for the footman, Thomas. "Shall I announce you to your father?" was his next question. "I believe he is working in his office."

"No need for that kind of formality. I will just find him on my own."

My response clearly disappointed Butler, but his training kept him from saying anything as he might have when I was a child. He merely pressed his lips together and inclined his head. He flinched as I patted him on the shoulder as I went by him. A glance over showed Thomas was fighting to keep his face stoic and free from emotion.

A laugh left my lips as I set off down the hallway. Maybe it was mean spirited of me to tease the servants as I sometimes did, but their general stiff bearing grated on my nerves. It seemed ridiculous even here in the country that it was necessary for the servants to behave in such a manner. After all, I had grown up with most of the younger servants—played with some of them, in fact— and knew them well.

Finding my father's office, I rapped my knuckles against the wood. A moment later I heard his voice call out for me to enter. "Hello, Father," I said with forced merriment as I entered the dark paneled room. It was a place I had always disliked in the house: far too dark for my tastes. "You sent for me, I believe?"

Father gave a start, lifting his gaze from the numerous papers that were scattered on his desk. His once dark hair was streaked with gray. I had inherited my height and stature from him, and he had managed to keep himself fitter than many men his age.

"Lucas!" he exclaimed, pushing his chair back. He rose and came around the desk to shake my hand. He embraced me, squeezing the back of my neck with an unexpected fondness. "Why did you not send word you would be coming home? I've been wondering if my note even reached you!"

"It seemed quicker just to come." Though I now towered over him, being six foot two inches tall, he still seemed larger than life. "Your letter followed me all over Europe, I think. It finally caught up to me not long after I landed in Plymouth a fortnight ago."

My father's face darkened at my words. "I'm certain traveling all over the world was not what your great uncle intended for you to do when he left you his fortune," he said as he returned to his seat behind the desk. He gestured to the chairs that were across from him. "You'll find yourself bankrupt if you keep it up."

"So you have warned me many times before." I pushed down the annoyance that was an instinctive reaction. My 'fortune', as the family called it, was a mere 800 pounds a year. The majority of the sum I had invested on the advice of a few close friends and a barrister. What had remained, I'd used to have my own version of a Grand Tour. Despite my father's implications, I had planned it all with the greatest of care and was in no danger of finding myself cleaned out. "I have it in hand."

I was in no way a wastrel, though I did enjoy time spent with friends. A wager or two could not be frowned upon, especially since I made sure to honor all my debts as soon as possible. Every now and again I was purse-pinched, as they said, but no more harm was done than that!

"So you say, but how am I to know?" Father asked, hearing the pique in my voice. "You spend so little time at home, Luke."

Was that worry? If it was, it was an odd sentiment, coming from him. We were by no means a demonstrative family and his embrace when I had first entered had been an extreme display for him. "If I hadn't inherited Great-Uncle Bywood's wealth, I would be gone anyway, given how a second son must make his own way in the world." I tilted my head curiously, considering what might have been. "I think I would have liked the sea. Perhaps I have missed out on a life in the Navy."

If I had been meant for the navy, I would have begun at a young age. From the time I went to Eton, I had been given subtle hints to develop an interest in either the law or the church. I had given it my best effort but neither had interested me at all. The unexpected inheritance from my great-uncle had been welcome.

There had been so many cousins ahead of me I never would have dreamed I would be chosen to inherit anything at all. However, all of whom had managed to upset my great-uncle so much he had decided on me as his heir. Then, his death occurred before he could change it to someone else, if he had ever intended to do so.

"The sea? Ridiculous! You would have gone into the church," Father said, getting my attention once more. "Your mother would not have stood for anything else."

Barely keeping a grimace of displeasure from my face, I could only be glad my great-uncle's passing had kept me from that career. I had no inclination towards that sort of calling, though I had nothing against those who chose to preach and sermonize for a living. I enjoyed a book now and again, but I could hardly be described as bookish. In fact, it had taken all my charm and good nature to get through university without disgraceful scores.

"Well, I did inherit a fortune and did not need to pursue a career," I said, clearing my throat. No use arguing over a future that hadn't happened and wasn't going to happen. "I have a great deal to tell you, Father, of all the places I have visited."

"Yes, your letters were few and far between. Your mother worried constantly." Father shifted his gaze to the closest chair. "Will you sit down, Luke? I will get a crick in my neck if I have to look up at you for much longer."

Obligingly, I selected a chair to sit upon and then stretched my legs. There had been yet another note of disapproval in his remark about my letters and I wasn't about to let it slide. "I was only gone for a year, and I sent plenty of letters while I was away, letting you know where I was."

"Well, your mother still worried. I will leave it to her to ring a peal over you. You know we never approved of this expedition."

In fact, they had spent two months trying to talk me out of it. Father's insistence was that it would be better for me to invest the money in Bywood hall, which had been a ridiculous suggestion. I had wanted to see the world and I had enjoyed every minute of my travels. If the war with Napoleon hadn't still raged on, I would have been interested in seeing Paris and the Parisian countryside.

"It was once the thing to have a Grand Tour," I said with as much mildness as possible. "I learned a great deal while I traveled."

"Yes, yes. I'm sure." Father waved his hand in a dismissive way. "A word now and again, more often those you sent, was all we would have asked for. But no matter. It's done and you're here now."

Which meant both of my parents were still unhappy with me but they wouldn't talk about it anymore now I was home. Fine with me. I cleared my throat. "I had meant to be back for part of the Season, but...well, sometimes travel can be unpredictable. Philly must have had a marvelous time while she was in London. Did she get swept off her feet by some worthy gentleman?"

Father shook his head at me. "Yes. Philippa accepted the offer of a respectable young man by the name of Bartholomew

Talbot. They are to be married this autumn once he comes into his inheritance."

"Good for Philly," I said with a smile. My younger sister could be a joy to be around, when she was in a good mood, and any gentleman who had earned her hand was to be congratulated. "I suppose you must be glad to have the last girl finally taken off of your hands. No more Seasons in London to sponsor."

"Lucas Bywood, you may keep such comments to yourself. I suppose you haven't heard the other news either. Your brother is married now. He and his wife returned from their wedding trip just a few days ago."

"George is married? This is news! Who is the poor girl he's been leg shackled to?"

"Again, Lucas, mind your tongue. He married a young lady of wealth and family who he met in London this Season, a Miss Rosamund Lamotte. I expect you to treat her with kindness. She's a sweet girl."

Holding up my hand as though swearing a vow, I said, "I will be the model of a proper gentleman and treat her as my sister."

"That's hardly reassuring, Lucas. I've seen how you choose to tease your sisters."

"Oh, fine then. I will treat her better than my sisters. But you didn't summon me from my journeys just to tell me the family news, did you?" Civil conversation with my father was a rarity and I had almost forgotten why I had returned home.

Something in my father's expression changed right before he glanced down at his papers. "Right. Well. There's time enough for that later. You've only just arrived and haven't even cleaned yourself up from your journey. You must do so before supper or you will offend the ladies."

"Oh, Mama won't mind the smell of the stable, as she will undoubtedly smell of it herself before she dresses for dinner. I will just wait until then to get cleaned up. I did not get too dusty on the ride here."

While Father was a superb horseman, it was Mother who had instilled the love of riding in me and my older siblings. My fondest memory of her was of her on her horse, laughing at the sheer joy of riding. She would rather be outdoors on the back of her beloved Sprite than sit by the fireside with needlework in her hand.

His lips flattened into something bordering on anger for only a second, but I didn't miss it. "Is there something wrong, Father?" I asked, feeling the worry that had begun to subside come surging back.

"I'm afraid your mother took a tumble early this spring."

Chapter Two

Shocked, I stared at him. From his tone, I inferred Mother had been hurt rather badly. Why had we been discussing trivial things when this was the reason I had been summoned home? "Why was I not notified sooner?" I demanded immediately, struggling to sit up straight. "What happened?"

"It was an accident," Father explained swiftly. He heaved a slight sigh. "There was a hole in the ground she didn't see on her morning ride. Sprite went down, taking your mother with her. Your mother wasn't able to get free, and her left leg was broken. She has been in her bed since then, and the doctor doesn't think it likely she will ride again."

Breathing out, I sagged back against the chair. "Mother never to ride again?" Nothing about that sentence made any sense, and I shook my head at the horror. "Poor Mother! She must be devastated."

"Sprite's leg was also broken, and I had to put her down."

I flinched. That alone would have broken Mother's heart, and my mind began working out how I could fix it somehow. Barely a moment later, and I had just the thing. "Miles mentioned his father might need to sell Midnight Summer since she's aging. She would be just the mare to replace Sprite."

"Your mother won't be able to ride again, Lucas," Father repeated, his tone becoming stricter.

"Yes, I heard you, but she should have a horse she can visit and spoil every day," I said, becoming more enthusiastic about the scheme. "Summer is a sweet-tempered mare that could use a lovely place where she can live out the rest of her days in peace, and Mother will enjoy visiting the stabnles, even if she cannot ride. I will suggest it to Mother when I see her."

Father shook his head. "Slow down Luke. I don't want you wasting money on a horse that has no purpose or use."

I frowned at his tone. Had I not just explained the benefit of purchasing Midnight Summer? That seemed purpose enough for me! "Why do I get the feeling there is more to this than you have told me?" I asked, unable to shake off the suspicion that was growing. I tried to work out the timing in my head. "If she was hurt in early spring and it's now summer, her leg ought to be healed at this point. Enough, at least, that she should be out of bed."

"Lucas, enough."

"You still haven't explained why you didn't let me know about this sooner," I added. "I would have come home sooner."

Father's eyes narrowed. "I will have you know, Philippa penned some sort of note when it first happened. If you hadn't been traveling the world, I wouldn't have needed to send word in the first place, young man. It is not our fault you took yourself off so far."

Understanding dawned. "Well, then, that explains it," I said, shaking my head. "Philly is an empty-headed thing on the best of days. She may have penned such a note but no doubt she forgot to send it. I hope this Talbot fellow knows what he is marrying."

"Can you not curb your opinion?" Father asked sharply. "This is no time for your jests or levity!"

It was always like this with my father and I. Ever since I was first sent home from Eton, I never seemed to say the correct thing. George, the firstborn and heir, could do no wrong and I, on the other hand, did *everything* wrong.

Holding back a sigh, I gave up on the subject for the moment. I knew exactly where I could get the answers I wanted. "Well, if there's nothing else I should know, I will just go up and let Mama know I have returned."

"I'm sure Butler has already sent someone to inform her."

"Then, I won't keep her waiting." I pushed myself out of the chair. "I will see you at dinner, Father. Unless there was some other piece of news you wished to tell me?"

Was it my imagination or did he hesitate? He focused his attention on his papers. "Not at this time."

The whole conversation had left me more puzzled than ever. What other reason could he have to summon me if it wasn't to inform me of my mother's injury? I left the office and jogged up to my mother's bedroom.

My knock was answered with a faint appeal to come in, and I pushed the door open. "Hello, Mama," I called out, keeping my voice low. "I hope you are prepared to put up with your scapegrace of a son."

Sitting up in her bed, Mother held her hand out to me. Her appearance was frail and sent a shock to me. "How wonderful!" she exclaimed, though her voice was weak. "Lucas! I didn't know you were coming home! When did you arrive?"

"Just now, Mama, and I meant it as a surprise." I hurried forward to take her hand in mine. "And what is this I find now I am here, Mama dearest? Tell me how this happened."

She pulled me to sit on the edge of her bed. Her dark brown eyes, so like mine, scanned my face. "It was an accident, nothing more, and then congestion of the lungs stole my strength," she said dismissively. "But look at you, my dear boy! So tan from going about in the sun!"

"You look as though you need to spend some time in the sun! I have much to tell you about where I have been and the things I have seen."

Mama sighed with contentment, a smile curving her lips. "I had so hoped you would be home soon, but I insisted your father not pull you away from your fun. 'He's only young once,' is what I said. 'Let him get his wildness out while he can. There will be time enough for being steady and responsible once he's married.'"

I laughed. "There's enough time for me to worry about finding a wife. I'm only twenty-two, you know."

She tilted her head with a frown. "You mean, your father hasn't explained— Of course not. You've only just arrived. Well, no matter. You'll know all soon enough."

What? "You may as well tell me all now you've started, Mama." What was so horrible neither of my parents wished to actually tell me? "I promise you I am old enough to hear whatever it is."

Mama shook her head. "I want no part of it, and your father should be the one to explain what he has done." As if to distract me, she asked, "Have you seen Philly yet? I know she will be ecstatic now you're home. She has news."

"Yes, she found herself a husband," I said with a laugh. I wouldn't force Mama to tell me since it upset her. "Father told me."

"Philly will be quite disappointed she did not tell you herself. She was so looking forward to springing the news on you."

"Well, I shall feign ignorance until she reveals it and then display the greatest shock possible. Who is this Bartholomew Talbot? I've never heard of him."

Mother launched into a detailed account of how Philippa had met her betrothed. Bartholomew Talbot was the firstborn son of a well-to-do family and would come into his inheritance later in the year. He would have a small estate fifty miles from Bywood Hall and was accounted to be a respectable man. All useful information, but did nothing to tell me about the man himself.

After half an hour of conversation, I could see Mama's energy flagging, and it saddened me. When I had last seen her, the day I left for my journey, she had been the most active person in the neighborhood. To see her so fragile and fatigued was alarming. I stood up and kissed her cheek.

"I will leave you to rest, Mama," I told her. "We can speak more at dinner."

She shook her head. "I have not had the strength to come down for a meal for some time, Luke. We can speak again tomorrow after I have rested."

Worse and worse! How could she have become so weak and I had not been notified it was happening? Surely, after no response to Philippa's first note, someone would have reasoned I had not received it and sent another message. They could not have thought me so heartless to ignore Mama's plight, could they?

"Well, when you have a good day, I will carry you downstairs." Sitting in a closed up room did no one any good and a change, I was sure, would do her the world of good. "I cannot imagine how everyone has gotten by without you to make sure they mind their manners."

Mama laughed softly. "You all are of an age where if you did not mind your manners without me there, I have failed as a mother. Come to me tomorrow at one o'clock. I want to hear about the sights you saw in Venice."

"Nothing will keep me away."

She had already closed her eyes when I glanced over my shoulder. I was careful to be as silent as I could leaving the room. Then, I made for my room. The conversation with my mother had left me even more thoughtful and apprehensive than the one with my father.

Father hadn't mentioned she had been ill after her fall, which explained why she was not up and about now. Mama had taken tumbles in the past but they had never affected her to this degree. That she had not been eager to take me up on my suggestion to carry her down told me she was worse than anyone had hinted at.

"Luke!"

My younger sister's exclamation pulled me from my thoughts, and I lifted my gaze in time to catch a figure dressed in pale green. Philippa wound her arms around my neck, putting all of her weight on me. I reeled a few steps back as though I couldn't support her.

"You finally came!" Philippa said, squeezing tightly. Her wispy brown hair tickled my cheek. "I thought you must have been killed when you never wrote to me. It was too cruel of you to stay away for so long!"

"Hello, Philly." After a few seconds of her embrace, I disentangled myself from her. "That's enough of that. It's good to see you, brat."

Philippa scowled up at me. "I am eighteen now, Luke. You have no right to say I'm a brat." She smacked my arm, causing me no pain at all but the action seemed to make her feel better. "What took you so long to get here? It's been ages since I sent you the letter telling you Mama was ill."

I raised an eyebrow. "Father said you wrote a letter after Mama and Sprite fell," She opened her mouth, no doubt to argue the point, but I kept talking. "I didn't get your letter, and this is the first I have heard anything of what happening. Are you certain you sent the letter at all?"

"Of course I sent it! You cannot blame me for the lack of reliable mail delivery in foreign lands if you're the one who chooses to go there."

Waving my hand, I decided to let the matter pass. "Well, I'm here now," I said. She wrinkled her nose, surveying my appearance. "Do I pass muster or do you find me wanting?"

"You have not washed from your travels," she said, her tone judgemental. Her eyes widened in horror. "Please tell me you did not go into Mama smelling like a stable!"

"Mama is not about to object to the smell of animals, sister of mine. But if I am so offensive to your nose, I will go to my room now and remedy the matter."

Philippa looped her arm around mine and walked with me down the hallway, apparently forgiving me for any offense I had given her. "I am so glad you are here, Luke," she said magnanimously. "My first Season was such a success, and you will never guess what happened!"

Even if I had not been told, what she wished to reveal would not have been difficult to discern. "Let me guess. You wore a pretty dress of fine muslin, and you gossiped to all hours of the night? Or was it that you danced until dawn every night?"

"I'm not a gossip! No, Luke. I had no less than four offers, and I accepted one of them. I am to be married!" Her eyes sparkled with joy.

"I am glad you accepted only one of those offers," I told her. "Imagine what would happen if word got around you had consented to marry all of them!"

Philly scoffed at my teasing. "You are ridiculous," she said. "Can you not be serious for one moment? His name is Mr. Bartholomew Talbot, and he is quite the nicest gentleman I have ever had the pleasure to meet. I have high hopes of him joining the party, and then you will be able to meet him."

"Party? What party is this?" I asked, reaching the door of my room. I paused, my hand on the doorknob as I glanced back at her.

"Phoebe told me all about it. Her parents are having a grand house party in a week. They have invited several of our friends from London. Phoebe is thrilled about it."

I chuckled. Phoebe Ramsey was a year older than Philippa and was one of the silliest girls I had the misfortune of knowing. Growing up, she and I had done nothing but fight if we were left together for longer than a few minutes. As the older one, I had been scolded for not behaving better, an injustice I had never forgotten or forgiven.

"She didn't say a word about you coming. Did you even tell her you were returning home?"

Startled by the question, I frowned at Philippa. "No, why would I tell Phoebe Ramsey anything?"

"Heaven knows Phoebe cannot keep a secret," Philippa said with a laugh. "She will be pleased when you visit, though she may not appreciate the surprise. It was badly done of you, Luke."

Blinking, I tried to make sense of her words. "I doubt she cares about my comings and goings, Philly," I finally said, giving up on understanding her. "Run along so I can change."

My sister frowned at me for a moment and then shrugged in an unladylike manner. "Brothers," she said with a huff. She spun on her heel and called over her shoulder as she walked away, "You have no idea what a lady expects from a gentleman!"

She was as incomprehensible as ever. I put the matter from my mind and entered my room.

Chapter Three

A few hours later, I finished tying my cravat in a simple knot and surveyed my appearance in the mirror. My travels had instilled in me the value of looking one's best, without the affectations many gentlemen of my generation attempted. I sought to imitate the simplicity Beau Brummel emphasized, though I didn't have the same elegance that gentleman possessed.

Satisfied there was nothing untoward in my appearance, I made my way down to the drawing room. My family always gathered there before a meal. I passed a maid carrying a covered tray: Mama's meal. The thought of my mother eating alone night after night made me purse my lips. Something would have to be done about that!

I could hear my family, Philippa above all the others, long before I reached the doorway. When I pushed the door open, she was in the middle of demonstrating some bit of silliness she had done earlier in the day. Stooped over in a ridiculous position, she glanced over, and her face brightened with a broad smile.

"Luke!" she exclaimed as she straightened herself. "You look so grown up!"

"You are generous, Philly," I said with a wry smile. I faced the rest of the group. Father was sitting by the fireplace with my older brother, George, standing at his shoulder. "Father, George. I hope I haven't kept you waiting."

I'd arrived downstairs several minutes early so I was surprised when Father said, "I'm not the one to whom you should apologize, Lucas."

Turning, I took a moment to study the seated woman. Her appearance was nothing like the kind of lady I'd believed my brother would choose as his wife, though she was pretty by any person's standards. Her hair was blonde and curled around her face. Her figure was admirable, but it was the expression on her face that sent chills down my spine: one of judgment and disdain.

"You must be my new sister. I am delighted to meet you, ma'am. Welcome to the family."

She shifted her blue-eyed gaze to my brother, refusing to acknowledge my greeting. "Rosamund, may I present to you my younger brother Lucas," George introduced formally. "Lucas, this is my wife, Rosamund."

"No introduction is necessary, even if your rapscallion of a brother has forgotten we are acquainted," Rosamund said, returning her gaze to me. "Mister Lucas Bywood, I wish I could say it is a pleasure to see you again, but I know your scapegrace ways all too well."

Surprised by this greeting, I tried to search my memory. She believed we were acquainted? For the life of me, I could not remember having ever met her. There was something familiar about her face, though, so perhaps our paths had crossed at some point. Far be it for me to contradict a lady!

She could only have heard me described as a scapegrace from my family, but I could hardly believe they thought of me in such a way. I may have chosen my own course in life, but I was by no means a disgrace to the family as she was implying.

"My dear sister Rosamund —I may call you Rosamund, may I not?" I stepped forward, caught her hand, and brought it up to my lips. The shocked expression on her face almost made me burst out laughing, but I controlled my features. "I have no doubt you will ensure my brother lives with absolute propriety."

"What do you mean by that?" George demanded, bristling as he stepped closer.

Rosamund pulled her hand free of my grip. "Nothing at all, George," I said, taking a step back. I glanced around the room and commented, "How quiet it is without Mama, Jane, Celia, and Jo here."

My three older sisters had been married before I had left for my Grand Tour so I should have been accustomed to the reduced number of our family for dinner. Perhaps it was the lack of Mama that made me feel the change. The room simply felt darker than I remembered it ever being.

"Isn't that the nature of families, Master Lucas?" Rosamund asked primly. Her referring to me as 'Master Lucas' made my lips twitch. Only servants called me that and doubted she would appreciate the comparison. And why was she referring to me as if I were a child? "Children grow up and make their own homes. You will, quite soon, I am told, do so with your own bride."

"Soon, you say? I'm afraid you have been misinformed, Sister Rosamund. I have no intentions of settling down any time in the foreseeable future." I was amused by the notion until I saw my father's face. And George's face. And Philippa's face? Slowly, I stopped laughing when it seemed no one else was amused. "Have I missed something?"

"You are engaged to Phoebe Ramsey, are you not? I was told it was a settled matter between you."

"I'm what? Engaged to Phoebe Ramsey?" I repeated, looking from her to my father. I didn't like the note of delight in her voice. "I have never heard anything so ridiculous in my life! I don't know why anyone would have told you such a tale since there is not a word of truth in it. George, do you hear this? Assure her that Phoebe Ramsey is the last girl on earth with whom I would form an attachment."

"Lucas, we will discuss this later," Father said sharply.

I was about to mock the idea further but stopped at his tone. The first stabbings of dread hit me. What was happening? "But, Father, it is an insane notion. No one could believe such a tale, let alone repeat it!"

"Insane? I was given to believe it was an understanding of many years," Rosamund said. Her hand flew to her lips. "Oh, dear. Have I revealed a great secret? I beg your pardon, Papa Bywood. I did not know!"

Her voice was as insincere as it was possible to be. What was she playing at? Our acquaintance was only a few minutes duration, but already I'd had enough of her. I absolutely would have remembered meeting her! How had my brother decided she was the best life partner for him?

Philippa latched onto my arm with a forced smile. "Let's go to dinner." When I resisted, her eyes widened into a silent plea. "Come on, Luke. Please?"

Rosamund rose, took George's arm, and then they walked past me. "Father, what is going on?" I demanded in a low voice, ignoring Philly tugging on my arm. "What is it you don't want to tell me?"

"We will speak about this after dinner, not before," Father said with the firmness I had come to expect from him. "Now, take your sister to the dinner table. You're acting like a child."

Clenching my jaw, I spun on my heel and stalked out of the drawing room. Philippa had to half run to keep up. "Luke, slow down! I don't see what you're so angry about. I have done nothing wrong, so there is no reason for you to punish me."

At the dining room door, I paused and took a deep breath. "Sorry, Philly. I didn't mean to take my frustrations out on you. I just don't understand what is going on. Why on earth would anyone have believed I would marry Phoebe Ramsey?"

She sniffed and glanced over her shoulder. "You are forgiven. I don't understand what you are so upset about. You and Phoebe used to play together all the time when you were children."

"Play? We tormented each other. No one could possibly believe we liked each other even a little bit!"

With a scoff, Philippa let go of my arm and swept into the room. Pinching the bridge of my nose, I shook my head and followed her in.

Dinner would no doubt be memorable, and not for good reasons.

⸺●⸺

ROSAMUND AND PHILIPPA carried the conversation, mostly with comments on their mutual London acquaintances. George contributed now and then, but for the most part, seemed content to listen to his wife. Father, to my surprise, had little to say.

The food had little taste, and I was relieved when Rosamund stood up to leave. "Don't be too long," she said to George, sliding her hand along his shoulder. Philippa wasn't the only one who rolled her eyes, but she was not in my sister-in-law's line of sight, so I was the only one to get a glare.

Already, I had begun my plans to return to London and take lodgings there. Never mind the Season was over, and no one worth knowing would be in town. I didn't want to become any more acquainted with my sister-in-law than was necessary.

But first, I needed an explanation.

Father waited until the port had been poured and the dining room door closed behind Butler before he focused on me. "Your earlier remarks about Phoebe Ramsey were uncalled for, Lucas," he said, his tone disapproving. "She is a lovely young lady and would make any man a fine wife."

"That may be, and 'any man' is welcome to her." I struggled to keep my tone within the bounds of respect. I wasn't doing a good job of it. "Father, Phoebe and I have never gotten on. She has always been a silly girl, and I have no interest in making her my wife."

"I think you should listen to what our father has to say before you make any similar comments," George said in a low voice. "You may come to regret the things you are saying."

Thoroughly annoyed, I sent a glare at him. "George, I fail to see what this has to do with you." He continued to sip his port, seemingly unaffected and I shifted my focus back to my maddening parent. "It is ridiculous to imagine Phoebe hanging out for a proposal from me! I'm sure she has never even thought of me since the last time she saw me, just as I have not given her a single thought until now."

"Lucas, you need to calm down," Father said. "You are making assumptions without knowing the facts."

"Well, if no one will come out and tell me the facts, what else can I do?" I aimed my glare down at the innocent glass in my hand. "Will one of you tell me what is going on here?"

"Lucas, you know John Ramsey, and I went to school together," Father said, seeming to choose his words with care. A glance up showed he was leaning back in his chair, clearly about to embark on a tale. I stifled an impatient sigh, wondering how this all connected to the impossible notion that Phoebe and I were engaged. "Our families had been close for over a hundred years at the time, and we constantly marveled how there had been no alliance between the Bywoods and the Ramseys."

"It would have made sense," George agreed with an emphatic nod. Of course, he would agree with everything Father said. He was the favorite after all. "It is often done."

Father waved his hand. To acknowledge or dismiss George's statement? "John inherited Lamridge when we were twenty. All of his sisters had found matches of their own, though some were less than could have been hoped for. It was at that time we made a pact. We would see our children united in marriage and bridge our families together."

My jaw clenched, and I began to guess what Father was taking so long to get at. "And what does this have to do with me?"

"George, of course, would need to marry a young lady of fortune. John understood this and agreed it was only right. Therefore, we made a contract that my second son, if I should be blessed with one to grow to adulthood, would marry one of his daughters. I have the agreement in my office."

Though I had already guessed what he was going to say, it didn't lessen my astonishment. "And you didn't think this was something I should know before this?" My mind went back to the half a dozen young ladies who had caught my eye since I left Eton, Phoebe Ramsey most definitely not one of them. I could have formed a serious attachment with any one of them and then what would have happened?

"We agreed it would be better to allow you both the opportunity to form your own relationship."

I couldn't keep from scoffing. "All those times we were at Lamridge , and you sent me off to play with all the girls, it was so I would become attached to one of them?" I shook my head. It hadn't worked out that way and had only fostered in me a sincere annoyance that I was always in the company of the meanest girl I knew.

Time and again, we had ended up in some skirmish, and as a result, we both were left muddy by the time we were separated. Once, I even had a broken arm to show for it. At the time, I was proud I had given her a black eye.

Our parents were not so impressed or pleased with our actions.

"Phoebe is not the plain girl you remember," George said, getting my attention. I narrowed my eyes at him. How long had he known of this? Long enough to tell his haughty wife it seemed, but had he thought to tell me? No! "She's grown into a lovely young lady now. As Father said, she will make you a good wife."

"Beauty is only skin deep. How many pretty surfaces hide rotting buildings underneath?"

"Lucas Henry Bywood!" Father exclaimed, aghast at my assessment. "I do not like what traveling has done to your attitude. I will not have our friends disrespected in this house."

I finished off the port in my glass, grimacing at the burn that went down my throat. I reached for the decanter and glared when George pulled it out of my reach. "This whole thing is ridiculous. It is 1814. This kind of arranged marriage is ancient. No one goes along with this sort of thing anymore."

"The contract is legal and binding."

"I never put my name to it, so I cannot be held to this contract." Being summoned home to be told a marriage had been arranged between me and the female I disliked most in the world was not what I had been expecting. I wanted no part of it, and I would not be forced to throw my life away.

The palm of Father's hand landed on the surface of the table and made me jump. "As my son, you will obey me in this. Phoebe and her family have been waiting for you to become settled into a career these past few years before expecting you to provide for a wife. Now that you have your fortune, it is expected the marriage will take place."

"And what penalty is there if I do not?" As far as I was concerned, nothing on earth could convince me to marry Phoebe.

I couldn't miss George's flinch. "If you should be so disobedient, and I am certain you will not act in such a disobliging manner, we would be forced to pay a penalty of five thousand pounds to the Ramsey family," Father said bluntly. "Your refusal would ruin this family."

Shocked, I stared at him. "Five thousand pounds?" It was an exorbitant amount, and I wondered why my father had agreed to it so many years ago. Had he been confident his second son—me— would agree to this? And that led to, what was in my mind, an interesting question. "What would the Bywood family have gotten if there had been no daughter? What if Phoebe herself had cried off?"

"Phoebe is a good daughter and would never consider disobeying her father," Father said, his tone pointed. He paused a moment before he admitted, "Such a provision wasn't put in the contract. She understands the benefits of this match, even if you pretend ignorance."

Well, wasn't that more than a little unfair? "So, you're telling me your old friend trusted you so little he thought you might try to cry off from this gentleman's agreement you concocted between yourselves?"

Father scowled but refused to argue this point with me. "Don't try to put words in my mouth, Lucas. Now, the estate cannot afford to lose five thousand pounds, and I know you have spent a good majority of your funds on your travels. Avoiding the penalty alone should be incentive enough for you to make Phoebe your wife."

Those words sounded close to a threat, but I focused on the first bit of information my father had let drop. "Are you trying to tell me the estate is not doing well?" I glanced at my brother. Father had tried to convince me to use my inheritance for the family estate. Is this the reason why? "Did George need to marry that—"

And then I struggled to find an appropriate term for my new sister-in-law. Where I had gotten on well with my older sisters' husbands, Rosamund rubbed me the wrong way. George scowled at me. "Rosamund is a fine lady, Luke, and she is my wife," he said sharply. "Think well before you finish that sentence."

'Fine lady' was definitely not how I would have described my sister-in-law. I decided that I didn't want to anger my brother any further and returned to the matter at hand. "But is Bywood Hall in danger? How did that happen?"

Color rose in my father's face. "Investments do not always turn profitable, and fields do not always yield results. We are not here to discuss the accounts of the estate."

Well. If that's what he wanted, I was more than happy to comply. "I will not marry Phoebe. I will sell my investments, if need be, to pay the five thousand pounds. Then we can be done with the whole situation."

"And have you ruin Phoebe's reputation?" Father demanded. "You cannot be so thoughtless! The Ramseys expect this marriage to happen. Phoebe herself has waited three years for you to come around and has had to turn down offers from many respectable men. Consider her feelings! How do you think the neighbors will view this whole thing?"

The neighbors knew about this arrangement? "Was I the last person to know about this?" The idea distracted from my intention of laughing at the notion Phoebe could have feelings for me. The last time I had been in her company, she had ignored me. Hardly the behavior of a girl who had some affection for me.

"Besides, Mama wants to see you happily settled, Luke," George said. "It would make her happy to know all of her children were married before—" He stopped before he finished the sentence but I knew how he intended to finish it.

Before Mother died.

How dare he? Shoving my chair back, I got to my feet. I had had enough of the conversation, and I knew the only way to end it was to walk away. "I take my leave of you, sir. Goodnight, George."

"Luke, you cannot simply run away and hope you won't have to deal with this," George snapped. "You will never solve a problem doing so. You should understand this by now. Your 'Grand Tour' is an excellent example of how that works out."

Did he think I had traveled to escape some problem? What did he know about my travels? I hadn't told him a thing about it.

"Lucas, this conversation is not over yet!" Father said before I could demand an explanation on that point. "Sit back down and be reasonable."

"In case you had forgotten, I had a long ride today." I held firm to my resolve to leave the room. I would get my answers when I was sure I could hold my temper. "You have given me a great deal to think about, and I have no doubt we will discuss this subject further on another day. Good night, Father."

Turning on my heel, I stalked out of the room. I could hear Philippa playing some melody on the pianoforte and Rosamund speaking to her over the music. I had no doubt my sister-in-law would provoke me and my sister would only want to chatter about things I didn't care for. Leaving those sounds behind me, I walked to my room to escape my whole family.

The calm quiet I found there was welcome after the news I had just been given. An arranged marriage? With Phoebe Ramsey of all people? I had never heard anything so ridiculous in my life.

Never before had I felt the injustice of being the younger son. Everyone had such strong expectations for me, and it was impossible to live up to them all. I was not like my brother, my sister drove me up a wall on good days, and I felt as though I was a disappointment to my father. The only person who understood me at all was my mother.

And her health was failing to the point my family apparently expected her not to survive.

"What am I going to do?"

Chapter Four

After a mostly sleepless night, I rose as soon as the first light of dawn showed on the horizon. What point was there to lie about in bed and worry? I dressed and made my way to the stable, detouring through the kitchen to alarm the cook by snatching some bread to break my fast. The morning air was crisp, and I breathed it in, enjoying the scent of hay and feed.

The grooms and stable boys were already hard at work. I nodded at them as I passed, intent on reaching my destination. "Hello, old boy," I said when I reached Phaeton's stall. My horse bobbed his head in answer and nudged my arm, no doubt searching for some treat. "Did you miss me?"

All I got in answer was a huff of horse breath in my face when I bent to lean my forehead against his. Laughing, I patted his neck and fed him a small carrot that had also made its way into my pocket when I had gone through the kitchen. Phaeton crunched it as I collected my riding tack.

"I can do that for you, Master Lucas." One of the older grooms, the man who had taught me to ride, attempted to intercept me.

"I prefer to do it myself, this one time, Geoff," I said with a smile. "You have duties to see to this early in the day, and I don't want to wait. I've been away from Phaeton too long, and I want to run him."

With reluctance, Geoff stepped back but remained nearby, watching as I saddled Phaeton. "It was a bad day when Mrs. Bywood fell," he finally blurted out.

Surprised, I glanced over my shoulder. Was this finally someone who could give me some answers? "What can you tell me about what happened, Geoff? I know Mama is too good a rider to be caught off guard by a hole in the ground."

The groom nodded, his expression grave. "She is. Mrs. Bywood went out riding, as was her habit. I went about my own business, and a few minutes after she left, I heard the screaming. We all ran to find out what had happened. The mistress had only gotten as far as the road, and she was trapped under Sprite."

Sadly, I knew what it must have sounded like. I had heard the anguished screams of horses injured before and the bone-chilling sound would remain in my memory to my dying day. The thought of Mama's cries of pain being added to those of Sprite's made me shudder.

"I sent John to get the doctor and Roddy to get Mr. Bywood while the rest of us pulled the mistress free," Geoff continued, his voice troubled. "We put the mistress home in a cart and took her to the house. There was nothing we could do for Sprite and I put her out of her misery as soon as I could."

"What aren't you telling me, Geoff?" It felt like everyone I had spoken to since I stepped foot on the estate was trying to protect me from something. "Did you see the hole? Was it new? Had it been there earlier?"

Geoff nodded. "I tried to describe it to Mr. Bywood, but he wouldn't listen. It wasn't natural and placed right where Mrs. Bywood always jumps the south gate. She wouldn't have seen it when she approached, and she wouldn't have been able to avoid it once she was in the air."

"Someone dug a hole deliberately?" I demanded, horrified at the thought. Who would do such a thing to Mother? "You are certain of this?"

"When I went back to have a second look and collect Sprite's body, the hole was filled. The dirt was fresh. There could be no mistaking it."

Phaeton bumped his head against my shoulder, impatient for us to be on our way. Reaching back to pat his neck, I considered what I had just learned. "My father didn't believe you?" I guessed. Since Father had said it was an accident, I already knew the answer to the question. Geoff's nod merely confirmed it. "No one else noticed the hole at the time?"

"If they had, maybe Mr. Bywood would have believed me."

Taking a deep breath, I reached over to clap him on the shoulder. "I believe you." How well I knew the value of hearing those words from someone. "Thank you for telling me, Geoff. I will do my best to discover who did this horrible thing."

"Be careful, Master Lucas. You may not like the answer when you learn it."

He walked away before I could ask what he meant by those cryptic words. My first thought was that it was my father who dug the hole. "But that's ridiculous," I said to myself, leading Phaeton out of the stables. "If any two people loved each other, it's Mama and Father. There must be someone else to blame."

I pulled myself up into the saddle and guided Phaeton away from the yard. I could feel Phaeton stretching his head, eager to race. Knowing I couldn't think about Mama's 'accident' and focus on my ride, I pushed the new information from my mind to give my attention to Phaeton. I nudged his sides and off we went.

Keeping Phaeton from a full run for the moment, I went to the site of Mama's accident. I rode right up to the gate and studied it. Naturally, I knew I would find nothing of any use at this point, but I wanted to get a fresh look at it. Many times in the past Phaeton and I had jumped in the same spot, and it hadn't changed much.

Shaking my head, I guided Phaeton away. "Alright, boy. Let's fly!"

Green grass rushed under Phaeton's hooves as we crossed the pastures. I barely took in the sight of the growing fields and the wildflowers that were blooming along the fencerows. The smell of early summer was on the wind and was invigorating.

When I finally reined Phaeton in, an hour later, we had reached the pond that often served as the destination for a summer picnic. Ducks were swimming in the middle, creating ripples that stirred the water. A frog jumped from the banks into the water as Phaeton and I walked by. Birds sang all around me, and a cow lowed nearby.

Halting Phaeton, I gazed over the scene. Nothing could compare to the serenity of the country. As much as I had enjoyed the streets of Rome and the parties in Venice, I knew I would always return to where I had grown up. Or at least, someplace that reminded me of home.

"Olivia, come back! Where are you going?"

A woman's voice startled me out of my reverie. Across the water, I saw a young woman coming around a bush, following the path that led from Lamridge to the pond. She was looking over her shoulder and hadn't noticed my presence yet. A moment later, another woman came into sight, twirling a parasol.

One of them had to be Phoebe, and I felt a moment of panic. She was the last person I wanted to speak to. Then again, who better to resolve the matter of an arranged marriage than her? And being away from our parents would definitely be an advantage.

"Here we go, Phaeton," I murmured, patting my horse's neck. "Let's see what has brought two ladies out at this hour of the morning."

I rode towards them, certain they would hear my approach. The second lady hurried to the first lady's side the closer I came to them. I slowed Phaeton to a halt and dismounted a few yards from the pair. "Good morning," I said, pulling my hat from my head. I offered a bow, keeping Phaeton's reins in my hand.

"Lucas Bywood?" the second girl asked, sounding alarmed. "Is that you?"

Turning my attention to her, I frowned. Gone was the tangled hair I remembered her always having and no longer did she appear gangly. Her hair was arranged in a surprisingly elegant way, for her being on a country walk, with one curl on her shoulder. Her gown wasn't wrinkled or stained, but dainty and fashionable. Far too dainty for a country ramble, I was sure. Phoebe Ramsey had gone from an ugly duckling to a swan while I had been gone.

"Miss Phoebe Ramsey," I said to her directly. "You're looking well this morning."

"Thank you?" Her tone was uncertain, and she sent a wide-eyed glance at her friend. "I didn't know you had come home. Did you come with Mil—I mean, Mr. Russell?"

Her companion heaved a sigh and shook her head. I glanced at her as I frowned at Phoebe's use of my best friend's Christian name. "No, I did not," I answered slowly "I wasn't aware he was planning on coming this way."

Miles had initially started off on the Grand Tour with me but had left after a month in Italy. He had said foreign travel wasn't for him and had seen enough for a lifetime. He and I had met up while I was in London, though we had not had the opportunity to do more than acknowledge each other and share a few news items, which is how I knew about his father wanting to sell Midnight Summer.

That he was to come to Bywood Hall should have been the first thing he told me, shouldn't it? Had he been invited to the party Philippa had mentioned?

"Oh, dear. Olivia, this is Mr. Lucas Bywood," Phoebe said with a start. Her cheeks had flushed a bright red. She fluttered a hand in the direction of her companion. "Mr. Bywood, Miss Olivia Darkin. She and her aunt are here for my parents' party."

"Miss Darkin, it is a pleasure to meet you," I said, bowing again.

Miss Darkin made a brief curtsy, her blue eyes bright with curiosity. She was not as elegantly dressed as Phoebe, looking more at home in the country in her pale blue gown. Black hair peeked out from under her bonnet. "Mr. Bywood," she said with a pleasant smile. Her voice had a soft, musical quality to it. "I see you are taking advantage of the lovely weather this morning."

"I am. I must confess I was not expecting to see two fine ladies at this hour. What prompted this early morning excursion?"

Miss Darkin glanced at our mutual acquaintance, but Phoebe was steadily gazing up at the sky as though the wispy clouds were the most fascinating thing she had ever seen. "Is it so odd ladies would choose to walk at this hour?" Miss Darkin asked when it was clear Phoebe had nothing to say.

"Not at all. I simply hadn't expected to see anyone," I answered lamely.

She gave another soft smile. "Will you be joining the gentlemen for their competitions during the house party, Mr. Bywood?"

"I expect I shall," I said, though I had had no such notion in mind before that moment. I shifted my gaze to the woman my father expected me to marry. "Will it be a big party, Miss Ramsey? Do I know the other guests?"

It felt strange to address her formally. She had always been 'Phoebe' the entire time I had been growing up, among other more unpleasant nicknames I had bestowed on her. I'm not sure why I felt like I needed to adhere to propriety when I had never been so inclined before. Miss Darkin's presence certainly had nothing to do with it.

"Oh, isn't that lovely!" Miss Darkin exclaimed. She started for the edge of the pond, leaving Phoebe with me.

"Your friend is pleasant," I said to Phoebe. She steadfastly refused to meet my gaze as she stared in the opposite direction. "You must be happy to have another female of your own age in the house now your sisters have all married and moved away."

Even that statement failed to elicit a response from her. Unable to think of *something* she would respond to, I fell silent.

At long last, she brought her gaze to me, her eyes wide, panicked. "Please don't."

"What?" I asked, more confused than ever.

"Oh, dear, she's been telling me and telling me I need to decide how to speak to you about this," she said, wringing her hands together and completely confusing me. "Why couldn't you still look like the evil boy who tormented me?"

Evil boy? Me? When had I ever been the one to torment her? Resisting the desire to argue the point, I shook my head. "What are you talking about, Phoebe?"

"Now, you mustn't go into a decline over this or some such silliness," Phoebe continued as though I hadn't said anything. "And I don't want you to be mooning over me either. I don't think I could bear it."

"Decline? Mooning? What kind of novels have you been reading? Phoebe, can you be serious for one moment and tell me what this is all about?"

"I don't want to marry you."

After all my father's worrying about the money and saying Phoebe expected to marry me, this was all it would take to put an end to it? "You don't want to marry me?"

She shook her head emphatically, making the curls around her face bounce. Her eyes were suddenly shiny with tears. Was she crying? "Oh, you are upset, aren't you?"

A laugh left my lips. Maybe Father and Mr. Ramsey would be disappointed, but they couldn't argue with Phoebe and me both. "Of course I'm not upset," I assured her. "I had no intention of asking for your hand in marriage."

She blinked, and a frown began to form. "You didn't? Why not?"

"Because you and I would never have suited," I said bluntly. Did she expect it was all well and good for her not to want me as a husband but she would be insulted when *I* didn't want her as my wife? "When it comes right down to it, we would not have made each other happy."

Pursing her lips, Phoebe shook her head, and her expression was mutinous for a moment. "But you're supposed to be in love with me."

Who could have possibly told her that wrinkler? "I have to tell you I am not nor have I ever been in love with you," I told her seriously.

Phoebe scowled for a moment but then sighed. "I should be relieved, I suppose. I would hate for you to be mad at Mr. Russell. An estrangement between two best friends over me would be horrible. I'd never forgive myself for breaking up a friendship."

Biting my tongue, I kept from laughing. "Miles? Why would I be mad at Miles?" A split second later, I remembered her earlier slip up using my best friend's first name. "Oh. Have you and Miles formed an attachment?"

Phoebe's smile became bright. "He intends to offer for me," she confided.

"Then, I wish you both much happiness," I told her honestly. Though I couldn't see what had attracted Miles' attention. Phoebe's looks may have improved, but she seemed sillier than ever. "He is to join the house party?"

"Of course. He said he was staying with your family."

A frown creased my forehead. "Is he, indeed."

And Miles hadn't said a word about it when our paths crossed in London. Did he believe I was in love with Phoebe? I would have to put things right as soon as I saw him. Then, this ridiculous matter could be put behind us.

"Phoebe, we should return," Miss Darkin said, as she joined us. There was no sign of whatever it was that had caught her attention and prompted her to leave us in the first place. "I am ready for my breakfast, and I want to sketch some of these flowers before I forget them."

On impulse, I bent down and broke off several of the wildflowers at their stems. I offered them to Miss Darkin. "So you don't forget."

Raising her eyebrows, she accepted the small bouquet. "Thank you, Mr. Bywood," she said as Phoebe stared at us with open astonishment. "Good day."

"Good day, Miss Darkin, Miss Ramsey," I said, stepping back. I mounted Phaeton and guided him in the direction of home. As I rode away, I couldn't resist glancing over my shoulder once. My eyes connected with Miss Darkin's, for she had glanced over her shoulder as well.

It felt like a good morning indeed.

Chapter Five

George sat alone at the breakfast table when I strode into the room. I made straight for the buffet of food on the sideboard, my stomach reminding me that food was an essential part of living. "Where have you been at this time of the morning?" my brother asked, glancing at the clock. He tugged at his cravat, which was tied in a manner far too elegant for a country morning.

"I was certain Phaeton hasn't had a proper run since I left, so I remedied that." After I filled my plate, I then took a seat opposite him. I reached for the coffee pot, having formed an intense fondness for the drink while traveling. "It was good to get out and see the countryside. Just the way to start the day, you know. Fresh air. Sunlight. Invigorating!"

"If you miss our countryside so much, you should stop this traveling nonsense."

"What do you have against my experiencing the sights of Europe?" It was hard to be properly angry with a plate of food tempting you, but I was willing to give it as good a try as possible. "Honestly, George! This isn't the first time you have been negative about my taking a Grand Tour. Are you jealous you didn't get one?"

George gave a scoff, but refused to meet my gaze. "Hardly." He sipped his coffee and set it down. "But, don't you think it was irresponsible to go running off as you did? To leave the family and seek your own pleasure?"

"Irresponsible, how?" I spread cherry preserve on my toast and took a moment to savor it. "I have no estate to look after like you do, and no family to provide for. What else was I supposed to do with my inheritance? Leave it sitting there, doing nothing but accumulating interest, as everyone does?"

"You should do something useful, not racketing around foreign countries."

"Meeting new people can be useful. Just think, I now know many more people than I did over a year ago. Who knows when such connections might be useful in the future? One never knows when one might need the ear of a diplomat, or the advice of an Italian duke, or the pleasant conversation of a French lady."

George did not look impressed. "I can think of no situation that could call for needing any of those connections to solve it."

I chuckled as I picked up my fork. "That is because you lack imagination." I paused the conversation and dug into my breakfast. My brother didn't say anything as I ate, and when I happened to glance up, I saw that he was watching me. I swallowed my bite of eggs and asked, "Is there something wrong, George? It's far too early to have such a serious look on your face."

"I'm just wondering what you plan to do about Phoebe. She is waiting for you to speak, Luke. It is hardly the behavior of a gentleman to keep a lady dangling over something that is unavoidable."

That I had already resolved the issue made me grin. "Not to worry, brother of mine. It has been handled, and I have spoken to her. I came across Phoebe and a friend of her's, Miss Darkin, by the pond."

Relief filled my brother's face, and he rose to hold his hand out. "This is a relief! May I wish you joy?"

"I did not say I was marrying Phoebe Ramsey. I spoke to her, yes, but an offer of marriage did not leave my lips."

Eyes widening, George collapsed back into his seat and his hands fell to his sides. "You are not serious. How could you be so rebellious, Lucas? Did you not understand what this meant to Father? To our mother? To the Ramsey family? They all want this union to take place. Are you only concerned about your own happiness?"

"You and Father made yourselves clear last night." I finished my coffee and rose from the chair. "However, this is a matter that lies between Phoebe and myself. We came to an agreement. I am sorry it was not the agreement you were hoping for, but there it is. I don't want to hear another word of the matter."

Turning on my heel, I left the room. I had no doubt George would have continued with his older brother mentality and escaping him was the only way to avoid any more scolding on the subject. I had no intention of spending the morning listening to him go on about how I had just failed the family would be nothing short of tiresome.

There were more pleasant ways of passing a few hours, and I was determined to take advantage of them.

⸺●⸺

PROMPTLY AT ONE O'CLOCK, I presented myself at my mother's bedroom. She was sitting up in her bed as she had been when I saw her the day before. The curtains, I was annoyed to see, were closed, and the only light came from the candles by the bed. Her lips curved with a smile and she held her hand out to me. "Have you been out riding already?" was the first thing she asked.

"Of course," I said, taking her hand and squeezing it for a moment. "Shall I open the curtains for you? The day is beautiful and will brighten the space."

"That would be lovely. Thank you."

Before taking a seat in the chair that was now beside the bed, I went to the windows and opened the curtains wide. The afternoon sunshine brightened the room considerably. "The morning was too fine to ignore, so I took Phaeton for a run. I should have brought you back some wildflowers."

Instead, I handed them to Miss Darkin. What had I been thinking?

"Another time, perhaps," Mama said, reclaiming my attention from remembering a pair of laughing blue eyes. "Come, Luke. We must have a serious conversation now. Your father told me he explained the arrangement between himself and Mr. Ramsey after supper last night."

Her face had taken on an anxious expression. "Mama, you must not worry yourself," I told her. "The last thing I want to do is upset you about this, but I have handled the situation the best way I could think of."

Mama's eyes became apprehensive. "Never say you've offered for the girl!"

Surprised by her words, I frowned. This was not the reaction of someone who was anxious for me to be married as had been implied. "No, I have not. Phoebe Ramsey and I were never great friends. I don't see how that would change now that we are grown. She and I agreed we wouldn't suit."

She breathed a sigh. "Then you will not marry her?"

"No, I will not. But, Mama, what is this concern? George told me you wanted to see me settled."

"That's true. I do want to see you with your own family, Luke," Mama said, relief in her voice. "However, as fond as I am of the Ramseys, I know how you and Phoebe are together. You would not have been happy with her. I told your father his pact was a foolish idea from the start. He and Mr. Ramsey were frightfully foxed when they made the agreement, and they should have agreed to forget the whole thing."

I felt as though a weight had been taken off my shoulders. "I am pleased I am not a disappointment to you."

Mama leaned forward. "Luke, you would only disappoint me if you allowed your father and brother to pressure you into a marriage that would make you unhappy. I want all of my children to be happy in life. You are the only one who will know the kind of young lady who will be a good life partner, though I have some thoughts on the matter."

My mind, oddly enough, went to Miss Darkin. No! I just met her. There was no reason for my thoughts to keep straying to her sweet smile and intelligent eyes.

"However, a foreign lady would no doubt send your father into apoplexy," Mama continued. "Especially if it were a French girl."

Shaking my head, I again pushed Miss Darkin from my thoughts. "I can promise you no Italian or French lady caught my eye while I was away." At least, not in any serious way. Flirtations, naturally, had happened, but I wasn't about to tell my mother about any of them. "I was too busy seeing the sights."

"You are aware I know when you are lying to me?" Mama asked as her eyebrow went up.

My cheeks burned with embarrassment, and I cleared my throat. "Lying? Me? Whatever gave you that idea?" I said, striving and failing to maintain an innocent tone. "Anyway, let us talk about something else. Miles Russell will be here for the Ramsey's house party, and his father is looking to sell Midnight Summer."

Mama's eyes brightened. "Is he? I remember Summer. She is a lovely, sweet-tempered mare." A moment later, though, her face fell. "But, your father will say we don't need a useless horse. I will never ride again, Luke. The doctor has told me so."

"Now, Mama, you must not think like that." I was alarmed by how swiftly she had appeared to give up. "Even if you do not ride again, which I think it far too early to believe such a thing, you will be on your feet again. Why shouldn't you have a horse to visit every day? Midnight Summer needs a peaceful place to spend her old age and someone to spoil her."

Her smile sad, Mama twisted her head to the side and coughed into her handkerchief. It lasted for more than a minute. Alarmed, I poured her a glass of lemonade and held it out to her. Looking pale and shaky, she accepted the drink.

"Mama, what else does the doctor say?" I asked. "Besides, you will not be riding again, I mean."

"Nothing of any importance. I am to rest and conserve my strength."

But she had been ill for so long! At some point, shouldn't she make an effort to get up? "And how long have you been resting and conserving strength? When will you be allowed to use that strength?"

She gave a huff. "You mustn't fuss so, Luke. My health is not something for you to worry yourself over."

"Well, I must ask your pardon, for I will worry. I cannot see how Bywood Hall will survive without you to see to matters. You are the heart of this old place, you know. You are needed to oversee everything."

Mama waved a hand dismissively. "My dear, charming boy, if Philippa cannot see to things, then I have failed as a mother to teach her what she needs to know." A slight frown crossed her face. "Of course, your brother's wife will have taken over all my duties as she will inherit them soon enough."

"I wish you would not speak so." My worry made my tone sharper than was needed. I took a deep breath as she frowned at me. "I'm sorry. Why has George not taken up residence in the smaller estate? I would think he and Rosamund wouldn't want to start their married life off in the middle of our family."

Shaking her head, she handed the empty glass back to me. "Oakcrest was let out about six months ago. The tenants, Rosamund's brother and his family, have no plans of leaving for the next five years. Your father has a contract with them."

"Father and his contracts," I said with a sigh. There went my hope of having my sister-in-law out of the house. I was certain it would come down to either her or me, and I wasn't sure I could make my escape without causing too much fuss. "What do you think of George's Rosamund?"

"She is a good example of how each person can know who will make them happy," she said, her tone diplomatic. Her hands began smoothing the blanket around her legs. "Rosamund is not the girl I would have chosen for George, it's true, but he seems to be pleased with her so what can I say on the matter?"

"You're right." I noted the tiredness lining her face. I had meant to ask her about the accident but now was not the time. "I will leave you. But, I want you to do as the doctor says. Rest up, and at the end of the week I will carry you down to your sitting room so you can enjoy the sunshine."

My mother's smile became one of indulgence. "If you say so, my dear."

I kissed her cheek and left her to nap. I went straight to the garden, where I found Philippa picking flowers. "I hope you intend to send a bouquet of those up to Mama," I said, making her start in surprise. "She needs some color in her room these days. And I wish you would advise the maid to keep the curtains open in Mama's room. How a person is expected to be cheerful in such a dark room, I do not know!"

"Luke, you mustn't sneak up on me like that!" Philippa put her hands on her hips. The breeze shifted a lock of her brown hair into her face, making it hard to regard her in any serious light. "Are you trying to destroy my nerves?"

With a laugh, I tugged on one of her curls before I took a seat on the bench next to where she was working. "It can hardly be counted as my fault if you are inattentive when I walk up to you. But I am serious, Philly. Send flowers up to Mama, or better yet, take them up to her yourself."

Frowning at me, Philippa shook her head. "There's no need for you to lecture me. My whole purpose in picking flowers today was to arrange them for Mama. You see? I've got all her favorites."

A quick glance showed she did have the bright blooms Mother was fond of in the basket. "And the curtains?" I asked, determined to win on that point.

Philippa heaved an exasperated sigh as she curled her fingers around the basket handle. "Yes, yes, if you insist. I will warn the maids to open the curtains every morning unless they are ordered not to. Will that satisfy you? Though I don't see how you expect Mama to get any rest if it's as bright inside as it is outside."

"The light and flowers will do her a world of good, you'll see." I stretched my legs out. A daisy hit the side of my face a moment later. "I say! What was that for?"

"I have no idea what you are talking about." She straightened up, looking past me. "Oh, you didn't say anything about Mr. Russell coming!"

Twisting my head around, I spotted my best friend entering the garden. He raised his hand in greeting. "Well, I'm glad I'm not the only one who didn't know he was coming to visit," I said as I got to my feet. Moving forward, I held my hand out. "Miles! Nice to see you again. I hope your journey from London wasn't too strenuous."

"Absolutely not," Miles said with a strained laugh. He took his hat off and offered Philippa his deepest, most formal bow. "Miss Philippa, you look even more lovely than the last time I saw you. I hear I am to offer you congratulations."

"Thank you, Mr. Russell." Philippa bestowed a smile on my outrageous friend. She sent a glance at me, still with my hand outstretched. "Luke didn't tell us you were coming. Now I must decide how to punish him for springing this surprise on us like this, for I am certain you had nothing to do with this oversight."

Miles set his hat back on and shrugged his shoulders. "You won't be too harsh with him, I hope. Perhaps there's simply been too much happening for him to remember his best friend."

That implication that I'd known he was coming coupled with how he hadn't taken my hand yet was puzzling, and I let my hand drop to my side. Philippa shook her head and said "When you put it like that, I will be far kinder than he deserves. I'll make sure there is a room for you. Good afternoon"

As she walked off, Miles faced me, all amusement gone from his face. "We need to talk."

Chapter Six

M iles' grave tone set me on edge. Since we first met at Eton, he had never been of a serious disposition. His willingness to go along with anything and everything had made us instant friends, much to the exasperation of our teachers. We'd had some of the best times together, and it had been a disappointment when he had not come with me when I went abroad.

"What do we need to talk about, Miles?" I asked warily. He was a good two inches taller than I was, and more than capable of defeating me if we came to blows. Though I wasn't sure why I expected that to be a possibility. After all, he had only said he wanted to talk. "Why didn't you say you were coming when we met in London?"

"Phoebe Ramsey."

Right. I should have guessed. I nodded in understanding. He was no doubt still under the impression I was expected to marry her. "Ah, I see. You will be happy to know I spoke to Phoebe earlier today and everything has been set right."

"I want your word, you will treat her right."

Taken aback, I blinked as I tried to understand him. "Now hold on, Miles." I held my hands up in surrender. "I am not going to marry her!"

My friend's hands balled into fists. "I will not stand by and watch you ruin her! She deserves better than that!"

"Miles, you need to take a moment and calm down," I couldn't help but be surprised by his reaction and immediately went on the defensive. "No one's reputation has been ruined. She and I discussed the matter, like adults, and we both agreed we wouldn't suit. In fact, I had the feeling she was expecting *you* to be at the pond early this morning, not me."

Breathing out, Miles collapsed onto the bench. "She was waiting for me at the pond?"

"It certainly appeared to be so, and she mentioned you by name." I couldn't resist teasing him. "Never say you had a rendezvous planned and then didn't show up! Bad form, Miles. That is the last thing you do to a lady."

Miles' face flushed bright red. "It was wrong of me to plan to meet her, and I realized it this morning." His expression became sheepish. "For all intents and purposes, she was betrothed to you. I had no business arranging to meet her privately."

"Still, you didn't keep your word. A lady does not forget a thing like that." A panicked look came to Miles' face, and he sent a glance in the direction of Lamridge . I took pity on him. "She'll forgive you if you go over there now."

Vehemently, Miles shook his head. "At this hour, she will be out making visits, or at home with other people visiting her. I will have to go tomorrow."

Strange. He'd never been such a stickler for propriety before. Didn't he realize things were less formal in the country? "I didn't know you were interested in Phoebe Ramsey," I said, curious to know how the attachment had started. All I could remember was how when Miles would visit in the summer, he would help me plot against Phoebe and her sisters.

He waved a hand as though the topic was unimportant. "She came out this past Season with Philippa, you know. Since you weren't there to make sure no one tried to take advantage of two young ladies from the country, I kept an eye on them both. I knew you would have done the same if I'd had a sister coming out."

I couldn't tell him that since he didn't have a sister, I had never even considered the idea. I made a noncommittal sound and returned my gaze to where I could see the horses being exercised. "Thank you for looking out for Philly. I don't suppose you can tell me anything about this Bartholomew Talbot?"

"Well, he's too serious for my taste, but seems respectable enough. He was courteous and attentive when it came to Philippa. It wasn't a surprise at all when the announcement of their engagement was made."

"You're no more help than Philly." Philippa was my only younger sister, so a little bit of concern about her choice of marriage mate was only natural. 'Serious' and Philippa did not go hand in hand.

Miles stretched his arms and stood up. "I do feel sorry for dropping in on your family without warning like this. It was shabby of me, but I didn't even stop to think I might not be welcome. I'm surprised Philippa didn't scold me more for not giving enough warning so she could be prepared."

I waved his apology away. "She'll get around to it at some point. It's my sister-in-law you should be concerned with."

"Sister-in-oh, yes," Miles said, realization and something indecipherable crossing his face. "George married this year. Why should I be concerned with the likes of Rosamund

Bywood née Lamotte? She seemed perfectly amiable when we met, as you know."

"Amiable is not a word I would have chosen to describe for her."

Eyeing me for a moment, Miles shook his head. "Well, you're the one who danced with her."

Had I? Why didn't I remember that? Could that be why she was so angry with me? Because I had forgotten? No. That would be ridiculous.

"Anyway, I'm sure there will be no trouble," Miles continued. "I suppose I should get some training in before the competitions at the house party. Are you going to join me, Luke? Or will you concede defeat now?"

"Defeat? When the party hasn't even begun?" Finally something familiar. "You are certain of your sporting ability? I accept the challenge!"

<hr/>

IN THE STABLES, MILES and I spent over an hour practicing our boxing skills. My friend had more skill than I, as I had spent so much time abroad and he had practiced in London. The grooms were mostly amused by our actions, and every one of them found some excuse to walk past more than once.

Honestly, the exercise felt good, and though I wished I could pour my frustrations into each hit I landed, I didn't want to cause any serious harm to my friend. Even with the marriage situation with Phoebe sorted out, there were still concerns weighing on my mind. Namely, my mother's 'accident' that had ruined her health. How was I going to discover the truth there?

"Luke! What are you doing?"

It was only George's appalled exclamation that made me finally pause and wipe the sweat from my brow. Grabbing the shirt I had abandoned for our training, I said, "What does it look like we're doing, brother of mine?"

"You ought to be getting ready for dinner," George informed me in a sharp tone. I realized then his apparel was formal, which was out of place in the stables. "Our guests will be arriving soon and you look no better than a common brawler."

I frowned at him. "Guests? What guests? Why would we have guests when Mama is not feeling well? That seems highly insensitive, George."

"The Ramseys are coming for supper." George's tone was sharp with exasperation "They are as good as family. And Mama wouldn't want us all to become recluses when she has been ill so long. How can you be so oblivious to everything going on around you?"

Now that was an unfair statement if I had ever heard one. First, Miles didn't tell me he was coming to the country and intended on staying with my family. Then, my family decided to have a dinner party, and I was left in the dark until the last minute. I was starting to take it personally, and my patience was at its limits. "If no one tells me anything, how was I to know?" I asked. "Never mind. I'll be ready on time, George. Have no fear."

Shaking his head and muttering under his breath, George walked away. Miles' expression was guilty as he picked up his jacket. "I'm sorry, Luke. I know you said Mrs. Bywood would be displeased but have I truly come at a bad time? Should I move myself to the Crown in the village?"

"My father and brother are just under a great deal of stress at the moment," I told him. "And I am, as ever, the great disappointment of the family. So it is as it ever is, Miles. No need for you to spend money on a room at the inn. Philippa would be put out if you made her see to getting a room prepared for you and then decided not to use it. She would track you down and give you an earful if she doesn't box your ears first."

Tilting his head, Miles frowned at me. "Your family doesn't consider you a disappointment."

Sending a look of disbelief at him, I started out of the stables. The grooms had disappeared as soon as George had made his presence known and now they were creeping back to work. "They do, Miles, but don't let it bother you. I generally don't. I am simply used to being independent and only relying on myself."

"So when will you escape back to your foreign lands?"

"I do not, nor have I ever run away, Miles." Though I had in truth been considering escape options open to me. I suppose that explained why George accused me of running from my problems. The only thing keeping me at the Hall was Mama. "While I'm thinking of it, has your father sold Midnight Summer yet?"

Surprised by the sudden change of topic, he shook his head. "Not that I know of, though I haven't spoken to him in several weeks. Why do you ask? Surely you're not interested in an old mare like Summer!"

"Actually, yes, though not for myself. I think she would be good for my mother. A horse she can spoil and visit when she feels up to it. She may not be able to ride again but why should she not have a horse of her own still?"

"Of course. Now you mention it, I think it would be just the thing. I will write to my father and ask him for more of the details."

Reaching over, I clapped him on the shoulder. "Thank you, Miles. I should have said it earlier, but it is good to see you again. It feels like it's been too long."

He chuckled. "Even though I was prepared to challenge you to a duel if you didn't come up to scratch?"

Astonished, I stared at him for a moment and then laughed. "A duel? You mean a serious meeting at dawn with pistols kind of duel?" Miles's smile had faded, and he didn't show any more amusement. "You're serious. On what grounds?"

"On the grounds that you were behaving like a cad by making Phoebe wait so long. I assumed you might not have realized what you were doing and if I mentioned dueling, you would come to your senses. I didn't think we would really have to duel as I don't fancy being dragged in front of the local magistrate."

I stepped aside to allow him to enter ahead of me. "Yes, I agree, and that's why I am amazed you would even propose the idea in the first place. How could you think the threat of a duel would be the best way to get me to propose? It is a ridiculous scheme."

"I told you it was only if you didn't come up to scratch in a reasonable amount of time," Miles said over his shoulder. "I don't suppose you know where Philippa will have put me, do you?"

Butler was hurrying towards us, and I gratefully gave Miles over to his excellent care. Choosing to use the servants' stairs, I hurried up to my room out of sight of anyone. This trip home had been full of surprises, and I wasn't particularly enjoying it.

"Nothing will surprise me now," I muttered.

Chapter Seven

Knowing I was bound to be the last one to go down for dinner anyways, I took my time in getting dressed. Hot water had been brought up at some point, but it had already started cooling. It felt good against my heated skin. I cleaned myself up and dressed in a more formal manner than I would otherwise have done, making sure my cravat was tied in the mathematical knot.

When I walked down to the drawing room, I could hear the loud chattering of our guests. Feeling tense, I took a deep breath and let it out slowly. What awaited me once I stepped inside? I pushed open the door and slipped in as quietly as I could. Keeping close to the wall, I studied the group that had gathered while I was upstairs.

Mr. and Mrs. Ramsey were seated together, talking with my father and George. An unfamiliar older lady was sitting in a chair by the fireplace, listening to their conversation. Rosamund and Philippa had Miss Darkin with them in front of the windows. I was not surprised to see Miles and Phoebe together in a corner, their words too quiet to be overheard.

"Luke!" Mr. Ramsey spotted me first. He seemed delighted to see me, making me wonder if Phoebe had explained I was not going to be marrying his daughter. "It's about time you returned to us, though I daresay your travels have done you no harm for here you are looking very well indeed!"

"Isn't it strange how people, in general, are surprised when someone returns from a journey looking well?" I commented as I moved further into the room. Out of the corner of my eye, I watched George's face turn red with barely controlled anger. "I cannot think of anyone who has come to harm while traveling."

An amazed expression crossed Mr. Ramsey's face. "Too true, my dear boy, too true. That is well said, my boy."

"Mrs. Darkin, this is Lucas Bywood, the youngest son," Mrs. Ramsey said, leaning closer to the lady I did not recognize. I offered my smoothest bow. "Luke, this is Mrs. Henry Darkin. She and her niece are here for our house party."

Mrs. Darkin nodded, her smile polite. "My niece mentioned she had met you this morning, Mr. Bywood."

"It is a pleasure to meet you, Mrs. Darkin," I told her. "I hope you had a pleasant journey here."

Father, however, was just as displeased by me as my brother had been. "There is always the threat of highwaymen to consider, Lucas," he said, interrupting me from exchanging any more pleasantries with Mrs. Darkin. "One never knows when one's carriage may be stopped by ruffians."

"I thank you for the reminder, Father" Although I thought I maintained an amiable tone, my father's eyes narrowed. "But such an occurrence, as rare as it generally is accepted to be, is easily dealt with if it happens, you know. Simply cooperate with said ruffians, and no one will be hurt."

"How ungallant you are, Lucas," Rosamund said, her tone chiding as she stepped up beside George. She looped her arm around her husband's in a proprietary way. "Surely, you would defend yourself and your wife better than that."

Even the sound of her voice made my back stiffen now. "Ah, but I am not married at the moment, dear sister." Her lips thinned into a straight line, and I was delighted to have annoyed her. "And even if I did happen to be traveling with a wife, resisting a highwayman who would surely have a gun pointed at me or someone with me would only result in someone being seriously hurt. I would not countenance such a thing happening in my presence."

"You are wise for your age, Luke," Mrs. Ramsey said to me. "I believe you would always do what was best for yourself and for any young lady fortunate enough to be your wife."

She sent a pointed look to where Phoebe was laughing at something Miles had said to her. Father gave a nod, though his expression was one of annoyance. "I would not say a lady would be fortunate to be attached to me," I said thoughtfully. "Unless she enjoys traveling and seeing the world, that is. Then, I would believe we would be fortunate to have found each other."

Alarm filled Mrs. Ramsey's eyes as her husband answered, "Surely, you don't intend on returning to those foreign lands! What can you possibly find there that you cannot find here, besides a great deal of trouble?"

"That is exactly my plan, sir! At some point, the war with Napoleon will be over and I fully intend on touring France. I daresay it would be no more dangerous in other countries than it is to travel through England. There is plenty to discover in the world, and I look forward to seeing more of it in the future. Egypt has always fascinated me and I would like to see it for myself."

"Lucas jests, of course," Father was quick to assure them.

"Indeed, I do not jest, Father." I glanced around and realized I had become the center of attention. "As I said, there is much to see outside of our country. I'm not surprised that taking a Grand Tour was once recommended for all young men of my age. It broadens one's horizons."

My father's face had become a peculiar shade of red. I counted it as fortunate that dinner was announced a moment later. "We are an unbalanced group tonight but what does that matter among friends?" Father said as he held his arm out to Mrs. Darkin. "Lucas, you will escort Phoebe."

I bit the side of my cheek. The last thing I required was a reminder on how to conduct myself as though I were a boy! Casting a distressed look at Miles, Phoebe accepted my arm and Miles fell into step behind us with Miss Darkin. Philippa was left to trail behind.

Why had no one mentioned this dinner all day since it had obviously been planned? My seat was between Phoebe and Mrs. Darkin with Miss Darkin across from me. Not necessarily where I wished to be, but I determined I could make it work.

"Before we begin, shall we start off with a toast," Father said, raising his voice to be heard by all at the table. He raised his glass, and everyone else followed suit. "To the future. May our families one day be connected."

There was a chorus of "to the future" but I couldn't bring myself to join in. To do so would indicate I *agreed* with what my father had said, and I most definitely did not. I had different plans for my future, even if my family did not agree with any of them.

The Ramseys were beaming and nodding in agreement. Phoebe refused to meet my gaze, and the stare Miles aimed at me was filled with betrayal. Miss Darkin frowned at her friend, though her aunt appeared to be oblivious.

I had no doubt my expression held exasperation. Phoebe had been emphatic about having no desire to marry me. Why hadn't she made that clear to her parents already? Why let either side remain hopeful for a situation that would never happen.

"I cannot think of a connection that would be more beneficial for everyone involved," Rosamund said from where she presided as hostess. I focused on her, unsurprised by her apparent delight in the whole thing. Why was she so anxious to see me wed? There was nothing to benefit her.

"I must say, I believe his time away has given Luke steadiness of character," Mrs. Ramsey commented. "It's wonderful to see. You must be proud of him."

Whatever Father said in response was lost to me. Miss Darkin caught my eye and raised her glass. "May I take wine with you?" she asked. Automatically, I raised my glass in return and took a sip as she did. The age-old way of expressing friendship did nothing to appease my annoyance. She offered a sympathetic smile before turning to attend to what Mr. Ramsey was saying.

At least there was one person who understood what was happening.

I couldn't follow any of the conversations that went throughout dinner. Any questions Mrs. Ramsey asked of me, I responded without hearing what was said or know what I answered. Miles glowered at me from across the table and Phoebe didn't say a word to me.

What was going on?

———◉———

IF MR. RAMSEY ASSUMED my eagerness to leave the table was because I wished to be by Phoebe's side, he would have been correct. But it wasn't a romantic inclination that prompted me to make a straight line to her and take her arm. I wanted to hear the truth and then strangle her.

"You are hurting my arm, you brute," Phoebe said as I pushed her to the pianoforte. "Lucas Bywood, let me go!"

"Choose some music to play, and I will turn the pages for you," I said, loud enough to be heard. In a lower voice, I demanded, "What did you tell your parents, Phoebe? I thought we had agreed we would not suit each other as life companions. Or did I misunderstand when you said you didn't want to marry me this morning?"

Pulling free, she scowled at me. Her back was to the gathered company, so no one else saw her expression. It would have suggested a less than lover-like feeling for me if they had.

"I had no other choice. Now go glare at someone else. I do not wish to speak to you."

I narrowed my eyes at her answer. "That has to be the most ridiculous thing I have ever heard." I set the music in front of her since she did not seem inclined to do so for herself. It would serve her right if she could not play whatever it was. "Why did you not tell them you have an attachment to Miles? Why did you have no choice? I will not marry you!"

A glance at my friend confirmed Miles was still glaring at me. "There is no engagement between us!" Phoebe insisted. Her voice trembled. "You don't understand what I have to endure."

"Be that as it may, the words 'I do not want to marry Lucas Bywood' are remarkably easy to say. You see? I just said them! And because you have *not* said them, everyone here believes we are betrothed!"

Her foot connected with my ankle and I bit back a yelp of pain. "We cannot talk about this now, Lucas. Someone might overhear and then where would we be? Meet me tomorrow morning at the pond. We can talk then."

She placed her fingers on the ivory keys and began to play. Sourly, I noted she knew the song I had put before her and took a step back, grimacing as my ankle pained me. Having no desire to watch her as a lover might, I shifted my gaze to the rest of the party and searched for something to distract me from wanting to murder Phoebe.

The older members had begun a game of whist, leaving the rest to talk amongst themselves. Miles continued to send dark looks in my direction. I had the sneaking suspicion I would be challenged to the duel he had mentioned earlier if I did not find some way to fix this mess.

Miss Darkin's eyes met mine, and she once again offered a sympathetic smile. What must she think of this whole thing? Though it felt good to have someone on my side in this situation, it appalled me that she had been pulled into it at all.

Tearing my gaze away, I focused on my brother and sister-in-law. George appeared to be telling some hunting story if his gestures were anything to go by. Rosamund's expression was bored which was an improvement over the cruel smile she had aimed at me through the whole meal. They were the most unlikely couple I had encountered, though Miles and Phoebe were strong contenders for the title at the moment.

I couldn't help but wonder what made Rosamund dislike me so much when we had hardly spent any time in each other's company. I really could not recall having met her, let alone danced with her as Miles had said. Her persistence in wanting me out of Bywood Hall puzzled me. Yes, I could understand it would not be enjoyable to have your husband's family continually underfoot but the Hall was large enough and what else could she have expected?

"Olivia, you must play now," Phoebe said, getting my attention. With a start, I glanced over to find her already standing. I hadn't heard a note of what she had played. "You always entertain us so well."

"Certainly, Phoebe. You know I am delighted to do so," Miss Darkin said, rising from her seat. She took Phoebe's place at the pianoforte and glanced up at me. "Do you have something, in particular, you would like to hear, Mr. Bywood?"

"I am sure anything you choose will be wonderful, Miss Darkin." She was the one person in the room I did not feel some hostility against.

She arched an eyebrow. "That is high praise, Mr. Bywood, but you have never heard me play. You cannot know whether I have any skill or not. I might send everyone from the room."

"You strike me as the sort of lady who would not put herself forward to play if she did not feel capable of entertaining." She laughed softly as she sorted through the music and I sought some way of continuing the conversation. "Have you known the Ramseys long?"

Miss Darkin sent a brief glance at the younger members of the party. "There is a distant family connection between us somewhere, or so my aunt tells me." She set her choice of music up. "However, Phoebe and I have only been acquainted for about two years. I would say we are close. Or as close as we can be."

"Then perhaps you could explain to her—"

"Luke, you must join us," Rosamund said, interrupting me. "It is too wicked of you to be away from Miss Ramsey like this. One might think you disliked her."

Holding back from a sigh, I moved away from the pianoforte as Miss Darkin began to play. Miles walked past me to take my place, and I couldn't help but notice the tense set of his shoulders. If he did not confront me before the morning, I would be more than a little surprised.

Though the seat next to Phoebe was vacant, I chose to stand behind the settee where she was seated. Rosamund frowned for a moment and then her lips curved with a smile I didn't trust to be sincere. "I have a wonderful idea. We should dance. Philippa, you play lively tunes so well. Mr. Russell and Miss Darkin can dance, Luke and Phoebe will be partners, and I shall dance with George."

A more managing female I had never met. Dancing? "You will have to excuse me from your plans, Madame," I said to her. "I am in no mood for dancing tonight. Do not let me put a damper on your fun, though. George always enjoys a country dance."

George, in truth, did not enjoy dancing and he frowned at me for saying he did. "I am at your disposal, my dear," he said nonetheless. "I would not for the world have you think the Bywoods are a disagreeable family by nature."

The implication being that I was the only person being disagreeable. How dare he! "George! That is a terrible thing to imply!" Philippa said, her tone offended by our brother's statement. "If any of us is disagreeable, it would be you. Why must you tease us so?"

With her aim of throwing Phoebe and I together thwarted, Rosamund made no response to her husband's generous offer or Philippa's offense. Instead, she focused her attention on Miss Darkin. I glanced over and saw Miles turn the page for her. Seeing him do so irritated me beyond measure. What right had he to dance attendance on another lady while his affections were elsewhere?

"What a fine match they would make," my sister-in-law said, her tone thoughtful. I was immediately suspicious. "They both have dark hair. Imagine how wonderful it would be if they were to use the house party to become better acquainted and then Mrs. Ramsey may have the distinction of two matches being made."

Phoebe raised her chin. "Matchmaking never did anyone ever good, Mrs. Bywood, and interference, I have seen, often times ends badly," she said sharply before I could formulate an answer. "You may be settled but permit the rest of the world to make their own matches."

It was as though a tiny bird had clawed a cat. Rosamund appeared to be startled, and Philippa's eyes had grown as round as a dinner plate. At that moment, I felt a brief moment of charity towards Phoebe and was pleased someone had put an end to my sister-in-law's matchmaking before she could take it any further.

Was it merely that Rosamund was a newlywed and did not like having so many of the family on hand? Would that explain her eagerness to see me married and away from Bywood Hall? Or did she have some other reason to dislike me?

Miss Darkin finished her song, and we all applauded, though I once again hadn't heard a note of what had been played. She demurred from playing another song and abandoned the pianoforte to Philippa. "Does anyone truly wish to dance?" my sister asked as she sat before the instrument.

"Yes, let us dance," Phoebe said, getting to her feet. "Mr. Russell, you will not be as stuffy as Mr. Bywood and refuse to dance, will you?"

Me? Stuffy? My indignation fled, though, when Miles said, "I am more than happy to share a dance with you, Miss Ramsey. I can think of no other activity that would bring me greater pleasure."

That put Phoebe out of my hair. Rosamund's expression was as though she had sucked on a lemon and I couldn't hold back a smirk as I watched. George summoned footmen to roll the rug out of the way. Philippa warmed her fingers up, practicing a few scales. I stood out of the way, wishing for a drink stronger than the tea that was on hand.

"If I may say so, you appear to be out of sorts, Mr. Bywood."

With a start, I realized Miss Darkin had come up beside me. "I give you leave to say anything you wish to me, Miss Darkin. I suspect you know the details of this whole thing, perhaps even more about it than I do."

She hesitated and then nodded sympathetically. "I cannot explain or tell you anything, which I suppose you were going to ask earlier. Phoebe swore me to secrecy, you understand, and I must keep my word."

"I will not press you for an explanation then. I will have the truth from her soon enough."

"Miss Darkin, you simply must help Philippa choose the right music," Rosamund said with impatience. "Lucas may be disobliging if he wishes, but I will not allow him to keep you from being involved and entertained."

Offering a smile, Miss Darkin moved over to the pianoforte and picked up the selection of music. Did my sister-in-law think she would punish me for refusing to dance? Well, I wouldn't give her the satisfaction of seeing me discomposed. I gave in and picked up a cup of tea. As I began drinking, I contemplated when and how I could make my escape from this evening.

The evening would not be over soon enough for my taste.

Chapter Eight

When morning finally came, I was tense with pent-up emotion. The evening had dragged on, and I had done my best to avoid my sister-in-law. Doing so limited what I was able to participate in. The younger generation spent much of the evening dancing and the older members passed their time with playing whist.

When our guests finally left, I made sure I vanished before my father or brother could speak to me. I also didn't want Miles to plant his fist in my face, which is what I would have been inclined to do if I had been in his shoes. Of course, I didn't see how I would have ever been in a situation like this.

However, once I was in my bed, sleep did not come easily.

I had done nothing but insist I would not marry Phoebe. Why had she agreed with me and then refused to inform her parents of the truth? I couldn't face my family until I had the truth from the silly, infuriating girl. And the truth would have to be—I don't know what, but she had better have a way to get us both out of this predicament.

Grabbing a slice of bread from the kitchen, I hurried out to the stables. I'd sent a message, so Phaeton was waiting for me. I led him out and prepared to mount.

"Have an important assignation to go to, Luke?"

At Miles' voice and cold question, I gave a start and spun to find him only a few feet away from me. "Were you waiting for me or did you follow me out here?" I asked, watching him warily. His hands were curled into fists, and it wouldn't surprise me if he tried to plant me a facer. "I will wait if you intend to saddle a horse and come along. I suspect you want answers as much as I do."

"So you admit you are meeting with Phoebe."

"I never intended on it being a secret. Miss Darkin will be there as well, I'm sure. I suggest we not keep them waiting."

Scowling, Miles gave a brief nod and strode into the stable. Ten minutes later, we were riding towards the pond. Miles edged ahead of me as though he didn't want to be near me. As irritated as I was, I could understand his feelings on the matter.

The day was cloudy, which didn't help matters at all. The wind stirred the surface of the pond as we arrived. Phoebe and Miss Darkin were there, as I suspected they would be. Both of them were seated on the grass, and Miss Darkin was sketching something. They rose as Miles, and I approached.

"You're late, Luke," Phoebe said immediately. It still surprised me how lovely she was now she was grown, but her tone of voice reminded me I was speaking to my old childhood playmate. "My mother would be appalled if she knew I was meeting you like this. It is on your head if we are caught."

"No one's sense of propriety will be offended with Miles and Miss Darkin here," I said to her as patiently as possible. "I think you have some explaining to do. You informed me, most emphatically as I recall, you did not have any regard for me and did not wish for me to ask for your hand in marriage. I have said so to my own parents, so why do your parents continue to believe there may yet be a match between us?"

Phoebe's pout did nothing to add to her looks. "Phoebe, explain it as you explained to me," Miss Darkin said with more calmness than I could have managed. The sketchpad she had clutched her in her hands tilted slightly, enough that I recognized the scene she had captured. I was curious to have a closer look, but it was not the time for that. "You must tell them everything at once."

Looking away from the sketchbook, I faced Phoebe, ready to hear her explanation. She bit her lip though and wrung her hands together. "Phoebe, my dearest," Miles said, catching Phoebe's hands in his. "Why did you not wait for me? Do you think so little of me you did not trust me to turn things around?"

With a pitiful sniff, Phoebe pulled her hands free and threw her arms around him. "I am so sorry, Miles. I never doubted you, and it pains me to know I have hurt you so. I had no choice. It has been terrible! My parents have insisted that Mr. Bywood has come to claim me!"

Clenching my jaw, I faced Miss Darkin. "Can you explain what prompted this madness?" There had to be someone with some degree of sense I could speak to as it seemed most everyone else had gone insane while I was away.

Sighing, the lady nodded. "It all began yesterday afternoon. I insisted Phoebe needed to tell her parents the decision you both had come to sooner rather than later. After all, why put something off when you can face it head on? She was understandably nervous about this so I agreed to broach the topic over tea."

Her matter-of-fact tone of voice was a relief in comparison to Phoebe's dramatics. "A simple enough plan. What went wrong?"

"Well, I began to explain to my parents how repulsive it all was," Phoebe said before Miss Darkin could continue. She untangled herself from my best friend's embrace. "And I barely said two words before Papa said how pleased he was that my future was provided for because he couldn't see how anyone else would be right for me."

Miles' expression became offended. "It would not have been that difficult to point out the benefits of marrying Miles," I said when Phoebe paused to wipe tears away. "He is of good family and stands to inherit when his father passes."

"Don't you understand?" Phoebe said exasperation filling her voice. "In my father's eyes, my Season had been uneventful. I did not catch the eye of any one of any importance, and no offers were made."

I was still confused, and Miles objected. "No one of any importance? Well, that is not what a fellow likes to hear about himself."

Phoebe clutched his arm. "Oh, you know I do not feel that way, Miles. It is what Papa says."

"Why did you not explain your affections were engaged by Miles and you were expecting an offer?" I asked, trying to get the conversation back on track. Why had a Season ever been granted Phoebe if she was all but betrothed to me? Mr. Ramsey could not have expected a gentleman to offer to a girl who is already attached since it was apparently well known to everyone but me.

"Because I do not know when that will be!" she said, her adoring look turning accusatory. She glared at my best friend. "It is unkind to make me wait like this. You both are so mean to me."

In turn, Miles shifted his gaze away, guilt written on his face. "Out with it, Miles," I ordered impatiently. Why did I feel as though I had to pull every word of this explanation from them both? Only Miss Darkin had been open with what she knew. "Did you not come down with that purpose in mind?"

"Of course, but there is a good reason why I cannot at this moment. One I will explain to you later, Luke. Not in front of the ladies."

For a moment, I thought Phoebe would throw a tantrum to rival ones she used to have as a child. "In any event, I made the suggestion that if Phoebe's happiness were at stake, a different gentleman might be welcomed into the family," Miss Darkin said swiftly. "I'm afraid I only made things worse by saying it as I did. Mrs. Ramsey was alarmed by the notion and demanded to know what Phoebe had done to disgust you."

"I could not convince them it was not my fault and a lady had the right to refuse anyone she liked," Phoebe declared, somehow managing to sound both pitiful and defiant. "Which my father took to mean I am rebellious and disobedient. The next thing I knew, I was explaining how you and I had met in the morning and had agreed to pursue a courtship. I said we wished to keep it quiet until your mother's health improved, Luke."

And there it was: the whole truth. Her bit of pride at stating my mother's health as the reason to wait grated on my nerves. I ran my hand over my face and heaved a sigh. "I am sorry you felt pressured, Phoebe. However, you have to go straight to your parents and explain you made a mistake. I am not about to court you, and certainly not going to marry you because you could not tell the truth."

My decree made Miles brighten. I was eager to put an end to this conversation and then get his secret out of him. "But everyone thinks you will be courting me!" Phoebe said, her tone alarmed. "What will they think if I were to say it was all a mistake? They will believe you had taken a disgust of me."

If I had been ten years old, I would have smacked her for that. As it was, I found myself having to make fists of my hands to keep from strangling her. "If you will not tell them, I will, Phoebe. As I just said, I have no intention of spending the rest of my life with you to save you from embarrassment."

"You are the worst person I know! You are so unfeeling!"

Her trembling voice made Miles scowl. "Luke, this is not the behavior of a gentleman! Can you not see that Miss Ramsey is distressed?"

I wanted to point out that Phoebe's behavior was not that of a lady and Miles shouldn't be the one chastising me about my decision. Did he *want* me to marry to save Phoebe's feelings? I spun away to get control of myself before I lost it completely. This was swiftly going from bad to worse, and I had no idea what to do.

"If I might make a suggestion," Miss Darkin spoke up. "If Mr. Russell can arrange his circumstances to be able to propose at the conclusion of the house party, I don't see why Mr. Bywood and Phoebe cannot pretend to be courting for that time. I'm sure you will be able to figure out how to gracefully part ways then. No one will be able to accuse you of not attempting to obey your parents."

That had to be the most sensible thing said all morning. Phoebe stared at her friend in bewilderment. "I think I can manage to carry on a *pretend* courtship as long as it is understood there are no circumstances where I will marry her," I said, nodding at Miss Darkin. "But how will it be possible to break it off 'gracefully,' as you put it."

Honestly, though, I had no care whether there was an amicable end or not. It wasn't as if we were friends.

"It would be simple," Miss Darkin said as calm as ever. "You have already made an excellent start over dinner last night, Mr. Bywood. Mr. and Mrs. Ramsey were concerned when you spoke about continuing to travel with your future wife. All you will have to do, once the end of the house party draws near, is begin contemplating the advantages of living abroad."

"Miss Darkin, you are an absolute genius!" I caught her free hand and brought it up to my lips. "What would we have done without you?"

She gave a light laugh as she pulled her hand out of my grasp. "I'm sure you would have come to the same conclusion eventually."

"Oh, Olivia, you have saved us all!" Phoebe rushed to hug her friend. "I just knew having you along was a wonderful idea."

"I must leave now," I said, relieved to have the situation settled. "My mother will be waiting for me. She'll need an explanation for all this as well."

"Oh, you cannot tell her the truth!" Phoebe said instantly, spinning around to face me. "We cannot tell anyone else about this conversation. How could we manage to deceive everyone if we are telling this person and that person?"

The word 'deceive' made my stomach turn but it was the most accurate way to describe what we were going to do to our neighbors and family. On this point, though, I was not going to budge. "I will not lie to my mother, Phoebe. She deserves to know the truth."

Phoebe scowled and then heaved a sigh. "I suppose as she does not have any visitors, no harm will come from it since she couldn't tell anyone. You may tell her, Luke, but no one else!"

"Thank you for granting your permission." I turned back to the one lady I had any charity for. "And thank you, Miss Darkin, for your help with this situation. It cannot be how you expected to spend your time in the country."

"Very true," she said in a distracted way. I followed her gaze to where Phoebe and Miles were exchanging their goodbyes. I cleared my throat as I focused back on Miss Darkin as she continued, "At least this will keep things interesting while I am here."

An awkward silence fell between us. "I hope you find picturesque scenes to sketch while you are here," I said, nodding at her sketchbook. "A few places are pretty enough, but they are not easy to find."

I was babbling. Why was I talking about scenery? She blushed prettily and held the sketchbook behind her back. "I'm sure I will," she said. Her smile became coy, and she arched an eyebrow. "Is that a hint you would be the one to show me where these places can be found, Mr. Bywood?"

Clearing my throat again, I tugged at my coat sleeve. "Yes? I mean it would be my honor if you would allow me to do so."

She laughed and stepped away. "I think you will have to remember that you are courting my friend at this time, Mr. Bywood." She raised her voice to call out, "Phoebe, I think we both need our breakfasts now. And your mama will be wondering where we are if we do not return soon."

With reluctance, Phoebe moved away from Miles, her hand slipping from his with each step she took. She sent a dark glare at me as she went past me. When had I become the villain in her eyes? I bowed with mock formality in her direction, but her back was already to me, and she didn't see it. Probably for the best. She would have been even angrier if she had.

Spinning on my heel, I found Miles staring after the two ladies, an expression of longing on his face. I smacked his arm to get his attention. I hadn't forgotten his actions had played a part in this mess. "Come on, you have some explaining to do, Miles, and it better be good."

<hr>

WE WERE HALFWAY TO the Hall before Miles finally slowed his mount to a walk. I remained beside him, waiting until he said, "I don't have the ring."

"What?"

He shifted his gaze to me, a serious expression on his face. "It's a tradition in my family, Luke. I made a point to acquire my grandmother's ring from my father to propose, but now I don't have it, and I have to get it back before I can speak to Phoebe. I would be disowned if I were to break with tradition."

Just when I thought things couldn't be more ridiculous! "Are you serious? How did you lose it?"

"I didn't exactly lose it." His expression held guilt. He cleared his throat a couple of times before he said, "I used it as security on a gambling debt."

Reaching over, I grabbed his arm. "You did what? Of all the irresponsible... Why haven't you paid the debt and taken back the ring?"

"Don't you think I've tried? He refuses to see me!"

"So you're telling me before you can propose to Phoebe, you have to get back a family heirloom you used as collateral for a game of cards," I said slowly. He nodded, and I heaved a sigh. "Who were you playing with?"

"John Lamotte, your sister in law's brother."

The man who was keeping George and Rosamund in the Hall instead of having their own home. "Then, there should be no problem. A gentleman would never refuse payment for a gambling debt. We will speak to him together. Who were you playing with at the time? If need be, we can bring them here to resolve the matter."

Miles shook his head. "It was just the two of us by the time I lost to him. Everyone else had quit for the night."

Stableboys ran to take Phaeton and Miles' horse. I dismounted and started for the house. Miles hurried to keep up with me. "Luke, where are you going? Why won't you say anything?"

"I have said something. Give me a little time to consider what we should do."

"Then you'll help me?"

The relief in his voice was unmistakable. "Since I don't want to marry Phoebe and you insist you cannot propose without this ring in your hand, I don't see why I wouldn't help." Maybe, on another day, I would have felt more sympathy for him, but right then, all I wanted was for the whole thing to be done.

And I had to find some way to explain all of this to Mama.

He seemed to sense I was in an unsympathetic mood. "Would it help if I were there to explain all of this to your mother? She must understand why I cannot break tradition."

"No!" That was the last thing I needed. Mama was going to be upset about the whole situation and having him there would not improve matters. "It will be better if I do this alone and as soon as possible. Thank you, though, Miles. I appreciate the offer."

With a nod, Miles took off for his room to clean up before breakfast. I, on the other hand, made straight for Mama's room. A maid was just leaving. "Good morning, Mama," I said as I entered the room. My mother was seated in bed with a tray on her lap. "How are you feeling this morning?"

The frown she directed at me spoke volumes. She sipped her chocolate and then set the cup down. Her movements were precise and calculating. Standing at the foot of her bed, I felt as though I were five years old, being held accountable for some transgression.

"Is there something you want to tell me, Lucas?"

She only called me 'Lucas' when I was in trouble. "Yes, ma'am," I said honestly.

"Perhaps an explanation for why you lied to me yesterday?"

If anything, her annoyance with me had brought some strength back to her. "Mama, I swear to you I did not lie to you. I meant every word. I do not want to marry Phoebe Ramsey asnd have no intention of doing so."

"Then why did your father come in last night to tell me the 'good news' as he put it? He said that you would court Phoebe."

"Because there's been a bit of a miscommunication," I said, choosing my words with care. As simply as possible, I explained everything Phoebe and Miles had told me, leaving out the precise details of how Miles had lost the ring he intended to propose with. I couldn't read her expression as I spoke. "However, Miss Darkin has suggested how we can overcome this and I think her plan is an excellent one."

"Miss Darkin?" Mama frowned. She had nibbled on her breakfast while I made an account of it all. "You've mentioned her a few times now. She is a guest at Lamridge?"

"Yes. A distant cousin of the Ramseys, or so I was told. She and her aunt came for the house party."

Thoughtfully, Mama nodded. "And is she a pretty sort of girl?"

Startled, I coughed. "Mama, you cannot expect me to answer that kind of question."

For the first time since I had entered, Mama allowed a smile. "So she is pretty; otherwise you would have answered she was not," she said with satisfaction. She sipped her chocolate. "I would like to meet this Miss Darkin to learn her character myself."

"I think she would be delighted to meet you, Mama. Would you like me to arrange a time for her to come?"

Mama waved her hand. "I shall see how I feel in a few days, Luke. So how did Miss Darkin solve this crisis?"

"She suggested that Phoebe and I carry out the pretense of courting until the end of the house party, giving Miles enough time to recover his ring. I will continue speaking of the delights of travel until finally revealing I plan on making my home abroad, in Greece or Italy. Phoebe will object and that will be the end of the matter."

Frowning, Mama shook her head. "I don't like it, Luke. It sounds cruel to raise expectations in a family that has been our friends for years. And do you actually plan on setting up your home abroad? What will they think if you do not?"

The moral aspects had been weighing on me, but hearing them spoken aloud so bluntly made me cringe. "By the time they realize I will not live abroad, merely spend more time traveling, Phoebe and Miles will be wed, I hope." I watched the disapproval cross her face. "What else could I do, Mama? Actually marry Phoebe?"

Sighing, Mama reached her hand out, and I hurried to take it. "No, of course not. That would only make a bad situation worse. It does seem as though it's the best option, but I do not like it, Lucas."

Again, using my formal name. "I don't like it either," I said, squeezing her hand. I sank into the chair by her side. "I should have spoken to Mr. Ramsey myself. Then all of this would have been avoided."

"There is no sense berating yourself over what you might or should have done." Mama shook her head. "I suppose this is what you must do to resolve this, so no one is hurt. I am just amazed Phoebe Ramsey would be so insensitive."

"She is sillier than I remember."

Chuckling, Mama picked up the tray and handed it to me. "Perhaps she is. But cleverness isn't generally a wished for trait in young ladies."

I stood up and carried it to the dressing table to be out of the way. My mind went to Miss Darkin and the intelligence that sparkled in her blue eyes. "That's true, but I would not happy with a silly wife. I am sorry to have worried you over this."

"I was disappointed with you and angry for I thought you had lied to me." Another smile brightened her face. "But I suspect you knew that when you came in here."

She brought her hand up to cover her yawn. "I will leave you to rest," I said, leaning down to kiss her cheek. "Oh, Miles is writing to his father for the details on Midnight Summer. I believe you will soon have her to spoil."

Genuine delight filled her face. "Oh, Luke, you do cosset me so. Now find something to eat. I can hear your stomach grumbling."

Laughing, I walked out of her room. It was wonderful to see her looking more herself than she had before. Before I had time to reflect on it more, I found myself running into Rosamund, quite literally. "What are you doing here?" she asked, recoiling a few steps.

"My apologies, dear sister," I said, knowing how much it annoyed her. It was, perhaps, unkind to persist in irritating her but I honestly could not help myself. Not after everything she said the night before. A maid slipped past us both and entered Mama's bedroom, no doubt to retrieve the breakfast tray. "I was visiting Mama, hoping to cheer her up."

Rosamund's eyes narrowed. "How sweet of you." Insincerity rang clear in her voice. "It must ease her mind to know she will see you settled before—well, we won't speak of that."

Everyone continued to persist in implying Mama would not get well and I had had enough of it. "I, for one, am eager to see her recovered. I'm sure she will be out of her bed soon."

A patronizing smile appeared on her face, and she reached out to pat my cheek. "You are so naive. Hold onto your hope if it makes you feel better, Lucas. The rest of us will remain firmly grounded in reality."

I jerked away from her. "I suppose we shall see which of us is right soon enough, dear sister."

"I came this way to visit your mother. I feel as though I have been neglecting her these past few days, what with your arrival and then Mr. Russell. It does cause chaos when people arrive without any warning."

"She's resting now." Knowing how Mama disliked Rosamund made me want to shield her from my sister-in-law as much as I could. Her negative attitude would get anyone down, let alone someone in the middle of recovering their health. "Perhaps your visit should wait for another time when it would be more welcome."

Gasping, Rosamund widened her eyes in offense. "Why Mama Bywood is always pleased to see me. Of course, you would not know that, having been away for so long."

At that moment, the maid came out. She paused for a moment, looking nervous. "Mrs. Bywood requests you move along. She wishes to rest and the sound of you bickering is not conducive to peace."

Scowling, Rosamund stalked past the maid and me. "Thank you," I said to the young woman. She bobbed a quick curtsy and hurried off. Shaking my head, I walked away.

Chapter Nine

I should have guessed Rosamund would not take my insubordination without retaliation. George caught up to me at the breakfast table. "What's this I hear about you preventing Rosamund from visiting Mother? Do you somehow think you have the monopoly on Mother's time now you are here?"

"Certainly not," I exclaimed, both offended and surprised he would suggest such a thing. "I did, however, know Mama was resting and did not wish to be disturbed. While I attempted to explain this to Rosamund, Mama overheard and sent a maid to inform us to take ourselves elsewhere. If you don't believe me, you may ask Mama the next time you see her."

George scowled. "I don't see what you have against Rosamund, Luke," he said as he pulled a chair out to settle next to me. "Can't you see how stressful you are making the family with this petty disagreeableness?"

My appetite ruined, I put my fork down and pushed my plate away. "My petty disagreeableness? I did not set out to butt heads with your wife, George. We do not get on, and I suspect we never will. She has taken far too much interest in what I do, and I do not appreciate it. The decisions I make in my life are for me and me alone."

"She is merely concerned—."

"Concerned? She is a nosy busybody, which is the nicest way I can put it."

"Luke, that is what I mean when I say you are disagreeable. You hardly know Rosamund, and yet you call her names."

Rolling my eyes, I shook my head. "You wish to know the truth? Fine. I do not like Rosamund. I did not want to say anything because I know you are...fond of her." I mentally added the words *'for some unknown reason.'* "I do not care for her manner of speaking. Perhaps it is because we are unacquainted, but as I said already, I doubt further time with her will change my opinion."

"Rosamund is a true lady," George said defensively. "Why can you not see that?"

"No, our mother is the true standard for being a true lady. I can only hope one day I find someone who is Mama's equal."

George frowned. "One day? You do not think Phoebe is worthy of you?"

I mentally kicked myself for the slip-up. "Do not put words in my mouth, brother-of-mine," I said sharply. "I said no such thing about Phoebe's worth. She is a fine girl, as you know, but she is not like Mama."

"It's shabby of you to criticize her."

"As shabby as trying to arrange a marriage for me that I do not want?" I shook my head and decided to leave the topic altogether. "Why must we argue whenever we are in the same room? When I think of the fun times we had as children, I am ashamed we quarrel so often now."

It was true. He and I had been close as children. Perhaps it was the mental idea of it being the only boys against four girls. Once we were sent to school, though, we had drifted apart, each finding our own friends and interests. When he left school, his focus went to learning how to run the estate, while mine went to exploring the world.

Heaving a sigh, George shook his head. "Don't think you can use your charm on me, Luke," he said, though a familiar note of fondness had crept into his tone. "Mama lets you get away with anything and everything."

"She does not." An idea hit, causing me to grin. In a gesture of peace, I asked: "Do you feel up to some fishing this afternoon?"

Looking genuinely regretful, he shook his head again. "Rosamund has already requested I attend her on some visits today," he said as he got to his feet. "And Father needs my assistance on a few matters for the estate. I have no free time for frivolities."

Disappointed, I forced a smile. So much for reinstating the bond between us. "Another day then, George."

George started to walk away, but then bent low by my side. "Between you and me, I would rather be fishing."

"No one will hear it from me," I said as he straightened up. My brother clapped my shoulder once before he left the room. Picking up my coffee cup, I stared at the opposite wall as I contemplated everything that had happened in the last few days.

Since I'd received the message from Father I had traveled nonstop to get home only to learn of Mama's accident. It was only for her sake I was glad I had returned. Perhaps a fresh perspective on her situation, a positive outlook, would be just what she needed to get out of bed and reclaim some of what her life used to be. I would be willing to endure anything to see that happen.

I heaved a sigh as I acknowledged I was in for an uncomfortable time. I not only found myself in a farce of a courtship but also of having to find some way of aiding my best friend to retrieve a ring he should have known better than to risk on a wager, security or not. Add in the disdain of my new sister-in-law, and I was faced with what was sure to be the worst month of my life.

But if I had not come, I would likely have not met Miss Darkin. Her warm smile and sparkling eyes rose in my memory. To be honest, I wished to know her better as the house party progressed.

"There you are, Luke. I've been looking for you everywhere."

Miles' voice pulled from my thoughts, and I put a grin on my face as I shifted in my chair to face him. He had changed from his riding clothes to obviously old attire. "Am I to assume you wish to go fishing?" I asked, taking a guess.

"Well, I hardly want to be obliged to remain in a place I would be expected to converse with Mrs. Bywood any more than necessary." He sent a glance over his shoulder and gave an exaggerated shudder. "I thought you were being yourself when you warned me against her. After all, she was all sweetness in London. But she is truly awful here in the country."

"I told you—wait. What? What do you mean you thought I was 'being myself?'"

Miles gave a nervous laugh, glancing back again. "Nothing. Is the tackle in the usual spot?"

"Miles! Tell me what you meant!" I sprang to my feet. He bolted from sight, and I sprinted after him in close pursuit. "Come back here!"

I SPENT THE REST OF the week finding ways to avoid my sister-in-law. Fortunately, I had Miles on my side in this matter, and he was up for anything as long as it took us far from Rosamund. As a result, one day we rode over to the next county to watch a fight. To say no one was pleased with us when we returned would have been an understatement.

"I cannot believe you rode all that way just to watch a fight! What appeal is there to watch two men beat each other into the ground?" Philippa said as she searched the shelves of our library. The rain, much to my regret, had kept us trapped inside. "It is completely ridiculous!"

With a chuckle, I glanced up from the letter I was writing. It was fortunate Rosamund was not of a literary bent, for she had not followed us into the library. Miles was in a chair across the room, and there was a book open in his hand. From the way his head rested in his hand, though, it was more likely that he was napping.

"I can think of a few situations that are just as, if not more, ridiculous," I said. "Take, for example, the tradition of young ladies traveling to London for a specific period, all in the pursuit of a husband."

My sister scoffed as she faced me. "No one gets hurt during the Season."

"Oh, don't they? What about the young ladies who have some misfortune occur during the Season? Perhaps they do not have the funds to be dressed in the latest style, or they do not make an impression on the patronesses of Almack's. Or the young men who are taken advantage of by those more skilled at cards. You cannot tell me they are not hurt."

Philippa collapsed into the closest chair and leaned towards me. "But don't you see, Luke, those things are avoidable by all. A clever girl will be able to make it look as though she is dressed as fashion dictates, and she will flatter everyone who needs to be flattered. Young men should avoid cards as it is, so they can avoid their ruination."

"Philly, don't be a prude." I returned to my letter, intent on finishing it. My eldest sister, Jane, deserved a few lines from me to be informed I was no longer abroad. "It doesn't suit you."

"And do not think you will distract me from scolding you about the fight. I think it horrible you would go off and leave me to amuse myself."

And there we reached the heart of her annoyance. "Well, it's not the thing for young ladies to be seen at fights, Philly. Besides, you have more than enough to do here to keep yourself amused. If Miles and I were by your side every minute, you would be yelling at us both within an hour."

"Better you than someone else I could mention," she said, just loud enough for me to hear. So, Miles and I weren't the only ones having issues with Rosamund. Philippa raised her voice and continued, "Why should you be able to run around and do whatever you wish when I must wait to do things properly."

"There does tend to be a double standard." Struck by that thought, I lowered my pen. "Young men are raised to be independent, while ladies are expected to rely on a man, their father, brother, and, if they are fortunate, husband."

"Yes! Exactly! It isn't fair!"

Before we could discuss it any further, the library door opened and Butler stepped in. "Mr. Bartholomew Talbot has arrived. I've put him in the drawing room."

Instantly, Philippa scrambled to her feet. "Has Mrs. Bywood been informed?" she asked, an apprehensive note in her voice that caught my attention.

"I believe Mrs. George Bywood is up in Mrs. Bywood's room."

"Come along, Luke," Philippa said, her expression clearing. "I want you to meet my betrothed. Mr. Russell, you are welcome as well. It may provide more entertainment than what your book is giving you."

An air of wounded dignity hung on Miles as he jerked upright. "I wasn't sleeping."

"You were, but no one said a word about it," I said with a forced laugh. "Lead the way, Philly."

There was a bounce in my sister's step as she left the room. The sudden change in her attitude amazed me. She was genuinely fond of this Bartholomew Talbot, though all I had heard about him said he was her complete opposite. Whether I would see what had attracted her was yet to be seen.

"Playing chaperone was not my idea of how today would go," Miles said, keeping in step beside me. "I can't imagine anything more tiresome."

"Not even reading a book?" I teased, though I mostly agreed with him.

Miles glared at me and muttered under his breath. Philly ignored us both and pushed open the drawing room. "Mr. Talbot," she said, rushing into the room with hands outstretched. "You have finally come."

"Miss Bywood," said the tall man. He made no move to take Philippa's hands and bowed. "I trust I find you well."

"Better than ever now that you have arrived," my sister said to him, her voice bubbling with happiness. "You must, of course, remember Mr. Miles Russell. And this is my brother, Mr. Lucas Bywood, just recently returned from his Grand Tour. I've told you about him."

Talbot and Miles exchanged greetings, and then my sister's betrothed faced me. I took a moment to study him. His height made me feel small in comparison. His eyes were a strange blue-gray, and his hair was a sandy brown. His clothing was plain to the point of severeness.

"Ah, the younger Mr. Bywood," he said, his eyes scanning me. His lip curled for a moment. "I was not expecting to find you here."

"A pleasure to make your acquaintance, Mr. Talbot," I said with a bow. "What has my sister told you about me?"

Honestly, what was my family saying about me? What kind of subjects would prompt them to bring me into it?

"You must not make this about you, Luke," Philippa said, her tone scolding. I pursed my lips to keep from giving her the set down she was in clear need of. To do so in front of her husband-to-be, however, would not be appropriate. She gestured to the chairs. "Why don't we all sit down?"

Naturally, we did as she suggested. "And how did you find your travels, Mr. Bywood?" Talbot asked. "You embarked on your journey against the advice of your family, did you not?"

"I enjoyed my journey more than I had anticipated I would," I said, striving for a cheerfulness I did not feel. "The art in Italy is even better to view in person than to read about in a book. And, of course, the sights of Greece cannot be compared with anything else."

A maid carried in the tea tray then. "Fascinating," Talbot said in a tone that said he didn't think it to be fascinating at all. "It was always my opinion young men would be better off not spending their family's money on such an excursion that is merely for pleasure and instead such men ought to put that time to use in preparing for the future."

"And why is that?" Miles asked, sounding offended on my behalf. "It is, in general, thought to be just the thing to broadened a young man's view of the world."

"True, but more often than not, it leads the inexperienced down dangerous paths to their ruin."

Philippa's forehead creased with a frown, appearing alarmed by the conversation. Taking pity on her, I said, "Well, to each their own opinion. I have come to no harm, nor brought disgrace on my family. I spent a portion of my inheritance and caused no depletion of the family coffers. But let us speak of something else. Did you have a pleasant journey here, Mr. Talbot?"

"I did." He accepted a cup of tea from Philippa's hand. "It was refreshingly uneventful."

"I am so looking forward to the house party," Philippa said, choosing to change the subject once again. "Do you know who else has arrived at Lamridge?"

As Talbot faced my sister, I saw the stern expression on his face soften. "The Williamsons arrived yesterday soon after I did. Mr. Ward is also expected to arrive at some point today."

"Mrs. Ramsey invited Ward?" Miles asked in a surprised tone. "I thought she disapproved of him."

"He may have some rakish tendencies, but he can be amusing and agreeable when he wishes to be, you know," Philippa said with a laugh. "Phoebe claimed she did not know who would be coming, but I am glad to learn the Williamsons have come. The daughters are delightful company."

"I don't believe I have had the pleasure of meeting them," I said thoughtfully. "What sort of girls are they?"

My sister shook her head, her expression reproving. "It doesn't matter what sort of girls they are, beyond the fact they are sweet and agreeable," she said in a prim way that was not normal for her at all. She focused all of her attention on Talbot. "It feels like it has been too long since we last spoke, Mr. Talbot."

Their formality with each other was puzzling, most likely because I was of a more relaxed nature. "Well, there will be enough time for us to speak during the house party," Mr. Talbot said to her.

Leaning back in my chair, I watched as the other three conversed about minor matters. Philippa's enthusiasm was not as noticeable as it once had been, and Talbot's reserve lessened the more they spoke. Miles lost his bored expression as he explained some occurrences he had witnessed while in Town.

None of them applied to me for an opinion on the subjects, for which I was both grateful and annoyed. True I had not had the same awareness of London happenings, but I could have contributed with similar situations from abroad. However, I knew doing so would only create conflict, so I held my tongue.

Soon enough, Talbot set aside his teacup and got to his feet. "I will take my leave of you now. No doubt the first activity of the house party will take place in a day or two."

"Oh, must you?" Philippa asked, also rising. Miles and I followed suit. "You have only been here a few minutes."

"I have no wish to overstay my welcome, Miss Bywood," he said, his voice becoming stern once more. He nodded at Miles and then an even briefer nod at me. "Mr. Bywood. Mr. Russell."

Philippa heaved a sigh as soon as the drawing-room door closed behind him. "He will not be convinced it is appropriate for him to stay longer," she said, sinking back into her seat. "What is the point of being engaged if there is no benefit?"

I caught Miles' eye and then shifted my gaze to the door. Taking the hint, he invented the excuse of having to write a letter and left the room. I crouched down next to Philippa and took her hand in mine. "Philippa, I must ask you to refrain from scolding me in polite company." She focused wide, innocent eyes on me. "It does not reflect well on either of us. We are neither of us children and bickering hints at a poor upbringing."

"You started it!" was her immediate declaration.

"Philippa, I did not," I said in exasperation. "I was merely curious about what you've told him. Rosamund has already made comments about having heard about me, so I was curious if your Mr. Talbot had heard the same things as George's wife. You are the one who then said I ought not make the conversation about myself."

"My Mr. Talbot?" She leaned forward. "Tell me, do you like him?"

She hadn't heard a word I had said. Next time, husband to be or not, I would not let her comments go unchallenged. Sighing, I let go of her hand and stood up. "He seems respectable enough."

"Respectable? Is that all you have to say about him? You are impossible, Luke!"

I shook my head at her. "Philly, I just met him. A few minutes acquaintance is hardly enough time to form a lasting opinion. I will say he is of a serious disposition, but it appears he genuinely cares for you."

Philippa's cheeks flushed red. "You think so?"

"Yes, but you do not need your vanity appeased anymore so I will not say any more about it."

The door opened, and Rosamund rushed in. "Philippa, my dear," she said, brushing past me without acknowledging my prescence. She sat on the chair next to Philippa and reached over to grab my sister's hands. "I was just informed of Mr. Talbot's visit, and I am so sorry to have not been here for you when you needed me. Why did you not send for me?"

"I did not want to disturb your visit with Mama," Philippa said, her enthusiasm and excitement returning to her voice. "Mr. Russell and Luke were here to make certain propriety was observed by all. Rosamund, he has told me who will be at the house party, and you will not guess who will be arriving!"

I left the room without a word, leaving them to discuss the upcoming weeks of activities.

Chapter Ten

Despite the misty, gray weather the next morning, I took Phaeton out for a ride. The gloominess cast a different appearance over the countryside and did nothing to improve my mood. The night before my sister-in-law had been as impossible as ever, and Father had sided with her.

"Why can you not be more agreeable, Lucas?"

Father's words rang through my mind as I crossed the wet ground. I had disappointed him so much when I had objected to Rosamund's suggestion I negotiate to rent a property thirty miles away. Deep down, I know my father wanted what was best for me, but he and I were so different, I couldn't see how he would even begin to understand what was right for me.

"Halt!"

That sharp command brought me from my reverie, and I glanced about until I spotted the speaker. A man on a black horse came forward, a surly expression on his face. I reined Phaeton to a halt and waited until the rider reached my side.

"You are trespassing, " he said without a greeting, his tone accusing.

"Indeed I am not. This is Bywood land, is it not?"

My tone was sharp, I will admit. I was not accustomed to being challenged on land I'd explored for most of my life. The man sneered and shook his head. "While I pay rent, it is my land, and I may say who is allowed to ride here and who is not. You are a stranger to me, and therefore you are the trespasser."

So this was John Lamotte, Rosamund's brother, and my father's renter. His appearance was nothing like my sister-in-law with his dark eyes and brown hair, though there was a haughtiness in his bearing that resembled Rosamund's.

"I meant no offense, sir," I said to him, striving for a peaceful tone. "I have ridden these grounds for years. I am Lucas Bywood."

The calculating expression that crossed his face puzzled me. "I am John Lamotte. I've heard of you."

I didn't even bother trying to hold back my sigh. "I am not surprised. What have you heard?"

He chuckled, setting me on edge. "Oh, nothing too dreadful." I felt relief until he continued with, "Only how you have let an inheritance go to your head and now you refuse to be guided by anyone."

"Only that?" I asked wryly. The mist had shifted back into rain, and I could feel cold drops running down my back. "I believe you are acquainted with a friend of mine, Mr. Miles Russell."

Lamotte's eyes shifted away, in a manner that could only be described as 'guilty.' "We have met in passing."

"In passing you say? Miles mentioned there was a debt of honor he has been trying to repay."

"Your friend may wait upon my pleasure in that matter," Lamotte said sharply. Whatever interest I had incited in him vanished in an instant. "He may repay his debt when I say he shall. Now, I must ask you to remove yourself from my property or I shall not be held accountable for my actions."

Rougher than was necessary, he jerked his horse's head around and rode away. Annoyed, I guided Phaeton in the direction I knew was the property line of Oakcrest. I glanced over my shoulder to see the outline of Lamotte in the distance, watching me.

Why would Lamotte want to keep Miles from repaying him? It was not honorable to refuse payment for a gambling debt. Of course, my initial impression of Lamotte was that honor was not of great importance to him.

Every time I woke up, I was faced with more questions than answers; more irritations than enjoyment. I also had no idea how I was to get to the bottom of it all.

EVERYONE WAS THANKFUL when the weather finally cleared up later that day. An invitation to join the house party for the afternoon in two days time arrived soon after. George immediately claimed estate business would keep him entirely occupied with our father, though my suspicion was that he merely wished for some time to himself. Thus, it fell to Miles and myself to escort Philippa and Rosamund to Lamridge .

Wanting to have an option for escape if it became necessary, I followed the carriage on Phaeton. "Do promise you will not behave in your usual manner, Lucas," Rosamund said when I offered her my hand to assist her out of the conveyance. "We are guests here, and though you may have spent a great deal of time here as a child and view it quite like a second home, it would reflect badly on us all if you did not behave."

I couldn't keep from bristling at her condescending tone of voice. "My dear sister, I was not aware you were old enough to offer me such advice," I responded coldly. Our relationship was on a downward spiral, and I was tired of being polite. "If you would be so kind as to remember you are not my mother and even one of my sisters. Only they can exact such promises from me."

Her eyes widened and her nose flared. "Oh, don't argue, please," Philippa exclaimed as she climbed down next. A twinge of guilt hit as I took in how upset she seemed to be over the situation. It wasn't fair to her or Miles for me to behave as a fighting captain.

"You are abominable, Lucas Bywood," Rosamund said, ignoring Philly's plea. "I will tell your father and George as soon as we return."

"I am not a child to fear you being a tell-tale," I said in as mild a manner as possible. I offered her my arm, and she scowled. "Do remember that we are being watched, Rosamund. You will appear shrewish if you refuse my escort now."

That prompted her to put her hand on my arm, and we marched to the front door. I had no idea *why* she continued to act hostile towards me, but it was getting out of hand. Perhaps Mama would have advice on how I could smooth out this misunderstanding. No one could resolve problems like Mama, and only the concern for her health had kept me from confiding in her sooner.

Servants were on hand to take our coats and hats, and then we were shown up to the drawing room. There was a small crowd assembled there, and they could be heard long before we reached there. Mrs. Ramsey delightedly greeted us as soon as we were announced and then made the necessary introductions.

There was the Williamson family: Mr. and Mrs. Williamson, the eldest daughter Katherine, and the younger daughter Eleanor. Then, there was a tall, dark-haired man by the name of Mr. Ward, who had a more reserved air about him. He acknowledged the introduction with a slightly inclined head but said nothing.

The remainder of the house party was known to us: Mrs. and Miss Darkin, Mr. Talbot, and the Ramseys.

Philippa made a bee-line for the Williamson sisters. Rosamund settled herself with Mrs. Ramsey and Mrs. Williamson, looking a little unhappy about being with the married ladies. Sending a sideways glance at me, Miles approached where Phoebe and Miss Darkin were sketching a vase of flowers.

"Do you have any fine fishing spots around here, Mr. Bywood?" Mr. Williamson asked, getting my attention. "We were talking of having a little friendly competition this coming week."

"Indeed, sir. Mr. Ramsey has the best-stocked fishing pond in the area, as I'm sure he must have told you."

"No need to flatter me, my boy," Mr. Ramsey said jovially. He clapped me on the shoulder, a fond smile on his face. "After all, you already have permission to court my daughter."

I forced a smile and glanced over to where Phoebe was laughing at something said. I hoped he would be more concerned about her happiness and not forever blame me when this courtship ended. "I only speak the truth, Mr. Ramsey. The size of the trout in your pond far exceeds ones I have found elsewhere in the county."

"I hope I can see my girls settled soon, especially my Katherine," Mr. Williamson said as I breathed a sigh of relief.

"Can you tell me anything of Mr. Russell's circumstances, unless he has already formed an attachment to Miss Darkin?"

Mr. Ramsey spun around to see Miles point out some detail of Miss Darkin's sketch. "Not that I am aware," he said, though his tone was filled with doubt. "Miss Darkin does not have a great fortune. She will have to do better than young Mr. Russell to make a successful match as her brother has the unfortunate propensity to gamble. As Mr. Russell is of good family, though, he would be an excellent match for either of your girls."

Why the Williamson ladies would be better for Miles than Miss Darkin, I had no idea. I had heard gentlemen discuss the advantages of specific matches when I had visited London before I set out on my journey. It had always amused me to hear the pros and cons weighed. This time, I found it irritating beyond bearing, and I wanted no part of it.

But where to go? Certainly not to the group of married ladies!

I took a step over to the fireplace where Mr. Ward stood, his expression filled with pure boredom. "Is this your first time to this part of the country, Mr. Ward?" I asked to strike up a conversation.

"I am often in the country in the summer," he said. He examined me for a moment before turning his attention to the room before him. "Why waste time at one's own estate when it is much more enjoyable and economical to pass it at someone else's? No doubt you did much the same on your Grand Tour."

"Very true," I was forced to admit, however much I disliked the mercenary concept. "Have you been abroad yourself?"

"Not recently."

It was like talking to a brick wall. "Did you enjoy your travels? What places did you visit?" I asked, thinking an exchange of experiences would take up some time.

"I did not." Just when I thought he had said all he intended to say on the matter, he continued in a sharp, blunt tone, "I was told travel helped put unpleasantness behind you. I was misinformed. You will not find me prosing on about the advantages that can be had by traveling, Mr. Bywood. Look elsewhere for that."

That unexpected information took me aback for a moment. He seemed to be one who appreciated blunt honesty and so I responded in kind. "Well, I am not one who needs to be agreed with all the time. There must be some subject which you are willing to converse on. When deciding between the gossip of young ladies or the repeated ideas of older men, I tend to find any escape possible."

For the first time, Mr. Ward's expression became amused. "Mr. Ramsey has been bragging about your horse, Phaeton is it?" he said, his informal tone deliberate. "How would you feel about testing him against my Tesoro?"

'Tesoro' I recognized as the Italian word for treasure. Finally, something free of any obligations to anyone else. "I never race against an unseen horse," I said, seeing no reason not to be honest. "Shall we go out and compare them before we decide on such a course?"

"What a cautious and logical suggestion," Ward said, the faintest note of mocking in his voice. He straightened up. "If you have no objections, any distraction right now would be welcome."

Any hope of escaping unnoticed by the rest was dashed when Mr. Williamson asked, "And where are you two off to?"

"Mr. Bywood has expressed a desire to see Tesoro," Mr. Ward said smoothly, "and I must see this paragon of horseflesh that is Phaeton."

No objections were raised by our departure from the room, most of the occupants were only concerned with their conversation. As we exited the house and walked towards the stables, I glanced over to find Ward directing a rather curious look at me. "What?" I asked.

"You are not concerned Mr. Russell is attentive to Miss Ramsey?"

I sucked in my breath as I realized my error. Most people would have expected me to be right beside the lady I was to court. He could not have been the only one to notice I did not go to her side to admire and praise her sketching, or even to offer a greeting. I would have to be more careful in the future.

"Miles and Phoebe are friends," I said, trying to think quickly. "We played together as we grew up." Never mind such 'playing' had been more like open warfare than childish fun. "I have nothing to fear from him."

Ward scoffed. "A blind man could see it is not mere friendship."

Scowling at the implied insult, I came to a halt and snapped, "You have observed them for a mere few minutes, and you make such judgment on a matter that doesn't concern you? I will thank you for refraining from making such comments in the future. Else, you may find yourself becoming acquainted personally with the ground."

"Such a defensive response," he remarked with a slight smile. A moment later, he shrugged. "As you say, it is not an affair of mine. I did not come here to offer advice on courtship."

Feeling only slightly mollified, I continued walking. "I would have been surprised to learn someone with your reputation had come to do so."

He gave an almost bitter laugh as we entered the well-kept stables. "A person with my reputation? There is no need to mince words. I know there are some who describe me as a rake, Mr. Bywood. However, a man such as yourself, who has seen the world, must know there are times when a person is described one way when the exact opposite is the truth."

Words like 'rapscallion,' 'abominable,' and 'disagreeable' drifted through my mind, all words used to describe me. I cleared my throat in embarrassment. "My apologies, Mr. Ward. I spoke without thinking. I can only plead to being under a great deal of stress."

"If I had the misfortune to be in the same house as a newlywed couple and a newly engaged young lady, I would no doubt be feeling much the same. It is bad enough to be an independent bachelor and have every matchmaking mama out to trap you without adding in those who are in the glow of affection and matrimony."

"Exactly!" I said, relieved to have found someone who understood. Miles had always enjoyed the attention and never quite grasped the idea that it could be tedious and annoying to some. I reached the stall where my horse munched on grain and patted his neck. "Well, this is Phaeton."

Ward and I spent the next fifteen minutes discussing the lineage of our respective horses and the trainers we had used. I found my companion highly informed on the matter and enjoyed every minute. We agreed upon a race, setting the time and date for two weeks later at one o'clock in the afternoon.

Finally something to look forward to.

———————●———————

"LUCAS, I WOULD LIKE a word with you."

Those were not the words I wanted to hear the minute I stepped through the doorway. A mere day had passed since the official beginning of the house party at Lamridge . In anticipation of my race against Ward and his Tesoro, I had decided to exercise Phaeton early in the morning.

"Certainly, Father," I said with a sigh.

Father didn't say anything but simply walked towards his office. I shrugged off my riding coat and passed it off to Butler. I sent a rueful look at my boots, caked with mud, shook my head, and then walked to my Father's office.

I would not be in the good graces of the servants for creating such a mess!

That Father immediately sat behind his desk wasn't a good sign for me. "Is there something on your mind, Father?" I asked as I sat across from him.

"I received a rather strange note from Mr. Lamotte yesterday. He claims you were on the estate without permission."

Frowning, I leaned forward. Strange that it had taken the man this long to send a note. "Is that so? I apologized when he claimed I was tresspassing. How long will Mr. Lamotte be renting Fordson?"

My question seemed to surprise Father, and he frowned. "We have a contract between us for a length of five years. Why? Did you have an unspoken interest in the estate? I can see what I can do about breaking the contract if that is the case."

"No, I was curious as to how long I would be banned from riding Phaeton across the grounds. I was surprised to be accused of trespassing earlier this week."

"Mr. Lamotte wishes to have his privacy," Father said, waving his hand dismissively. "It is a bit of an inconvenience to be sure, but we have been working around it these past six months well enough. We must have mentioned this to you."

"No, you did not." I was certain I would have remembered such a detail.

Father seemed to sense my annoyance because his voice became defensive. "Well, you cannot expect us to keep you abreast of every change in the estate if you insist on doing whatever you wish. You are the one who left the country."

It always came back to my leaving. Sighing, I got to my feet. "I'm sorry to have disappointed you yet again, Father. If you will excuse me, I have an appointment with Mama, and I would hate to keep her waiting."

Father echoed me with a sigh of his own. "Of course."

I strode out without a word. As I did so, I caught sight of a rose-colored morning gown vanishing around the corner. Had Rosamund been eavesdropping? I clenched my jaw at the notion. She had become a constant thorn in my side, and I had no idea how I would be able to cope with her needling and interfering for much longer.

Chapter Eleven

To my surprise, I found Mama sitting at her dressing table when I entered her personal chamber. Her maid, Simmons, had just finished arranging Mama's hair and looked quite pleased with the work she had done. "There you are, Lucas," Mama said, making eye contact with me in her mirror. "You are right on time. Have you been out on Phaeton?"

"I have." My heart swelled with happiness to see her looking better than ever. "I don't think I've seen you so lovely. Well done, Simmons."

"Oh, hush." Mama's cheeks flushed with color and her eyes sparkled. "It's time to make good on your promise to take me downstairs. Not to the drawing room but the sitting room. I believe I will need your arm."

"Are you sure you feel up to it?" I watched her face for any sign of discomfort or hesitation. "Won't Rosamund and Philippa tax your strength?"

"Rosamund and Philippa have already gone to Lamridge ," she said, standing up. She kept her hand on her chair and seemed steady. I stepped over and offered my arm, which she graciously accepted with a smile. "There is an archery competition the ladies planned for today, so Philippa was eager to be there."

After a moment, I vaguely remembered my sister and Rosamund the archery competition the previous night, though I had been doing my best to ignore them both at the time. I helped Mama steady herself. "I'm surprised Philly didn't try to coerce me into going."

"I am glad she did not," Mama said no more as we slowly made our way to the sitting room. There was a distinct limp in her walk that broke my heart. She was pale and out of breath by the time we reached the sitting room. I seated her by the window where the sunlight would shine on her. "Thank you, Luke."

"Is there anything you need?" I asked, eager to ease her pain in some way.

"You might hand me my sewing basket," Mama said, gesturing to where the basket in question sat. As I retrieved it, she coughed, her shoulders shaking. "Thank you. One must always keep up appearances, you know. I would hate for it to get about that I was being lazy."

That statement raised my suspicions. "Mama, what are you up to?"

"Why must I be 'up to' something?"

"Because I know you all too well, Mama."

Her smile was enigmatic as she drew a piece of needlework out of the basket. "Suspicion doesn't look good on you, Luke," she said in her serene way. "Sit down. I will not give myself a pain in my neck looking up at you while we talk."

Collapsing into the chair by her, I bit back a frustrated groan. Silence fell as Mama untangled her thread and I watched her. "Mama, I do have a question for you," I said, taking advantage of the opportunity that had presented itself. She sent a glance towards me. "Geoffrey told me about the hole that caused you and Sprite to fall. Did Father say anything about it to you?"

Her hands went still for a moment, and I saw her frown. "Your father wouldn't speak of it." She paused to thread her needle and then continued, "Though you know he has never been pleased with my habit of jumping the gate. He was furious when he learned I had taught all of my children how to do it."

I chuckled as I remembered the day Father had discovered our favorite pastime. "And, of course, we taught Miles because it was the shortest way to get from here to Oakcrest," I said with a laugh. As the realization hit, my smile slipped from my face. "It was a shortcut."

"I have no idea how the hole ended up right in front of the gate," Mama said, focusing on her work. "The farmers use the gate all the time, and I know they would have kept it smooth."

She may have said more on the matter, but I stopped listening. Miles and I had *always* used the gate to get to and from Oakcrest. It would have been the only way he'd know to get there. Maybe the deliberate hole wasn't meant for Mama but Miles. He would have used it when he attempted to repay his debt to Lamotte.

"Lucas!" Mama's sharp voice brought me back to the sitting room. "What's wrong?"

"Sorry, Mama," I said apologetically as I shook my head. "I was just—thinking of something."

"I could see that." She set her sewing in her lap and leaned forward. "You appeared to be horrified, Luke. What were you thinking of?"

I had been warned before my emotions played out on my face, and nothing I did seemed to stop it. "It's nothing important," I said, anxious to keep her from being upset. Mama's expression of skepticism, her pursed lips and narrowed eyes, forced me to invent an excuse. "I imagined how Father would react if we taught Rosamund to jump the gate along with the rest of us."

Instead of becoming amused, Mama's expression became grave. "Rosamund, I fear, is not the sort of girl who would ever allow herself to be seen doing that." Anything else she might have said on the matter was cut off by yet another coughing fit. She waved me away when I moved towards her and straightened after a moment. "What's the time, Luke?"

Surprised, I glanced down at my watch. "It is nearly one," I told her before asking her a very important question. "Mama, was Miles here when you had your accident?"

She didn't even hestitate. "Why, yes, he was. Didn't you know?"

Shaking my head, I considered it carefully. None of this made sense. Wouldn't Mr. Lamotte want to get his money? Why would he try to kill Miles? Pushing it from my mind, I faced her. "Why did you want to know the time? Are you expecting someone?"

As if on cue, the sitting-room door opened. "Miss Darkin and Mr. Ward," Butler said before he stepped aside.

Delight filled Mama's face as she smiled. Shocked, I shot to my feet and moved forward to greet our guests. Miss Darkin and Ward? Why were they making visits together? "Miss Darkin, Mr. Ward. This is a surprise. Welcome to Bywood Hall."

"Bywood," Ward said in a bored tone.

"Good afternoon, Mr. Bywood," Miss Darkin responded with a charming smile that had been lingering in my memory all week.

My mother cleared her throat, reminding me of my manners. "Mama, may I present to you Miss Darkin and Mr. Ward. Miss Darkin, Mr. Ward, this is my mother, Mrs. Bywood."

"You will forgive me for not rising," Mama said, nodding in acknowledgment as Miss Darkin curtsied and Ward bowed. "Please, sit down."

I remained on my feet as Miss Darkin took the seat I had been occupying. "I'm surprised you both abandoned the house party. Neither of you wanted to watch the archery contest?" I asked curiously, glancing between her and Ward, who had taken up a position at the fireplace as he generally did whenever I saw him.

"I have no skill at archery, and I have never been in a position to fire a pistol," Miss Darkin said with a rueful smile. "Therefore, when I received your mother's note, inviting me to visit this afternoon, I was more than happy to oblige. Mr. Ward and I crossed paths while I was on my way here. As he had no particular plan, he was kind enough to join me."

Why hadn't Mama warned me?

"I am so pleased you could take the time to visit an elderly, sick woman, when most young ladies would prefer to enjoy the day," Mama said, ignoring my accusing look. "And you, Mr. Ward? Was there no young lady you wished to cheer on this afternoon?"

Ward's manner became tense. "There was not," was his answer. "I find myself unable to observe such a competition without being reminded of a young lady who would have outshone them all."

Now that was an interesting comment. Who could he mean? While I was mildly curious as to his tale, I was more concerned with why my mother had requested Miss Darkin come to the Hall. "How are you enjoying your visit to our neighborhood, Miss Darkin?" I asked.

"It is more interesting than I had anticipated," Miss Darkin said immediately. "The Ramseys have made sure we all are entertained every minute."

"Luke, why don't you and Mr. Ward find something to occupy yourselves with?" Mama said, sending a sharp look my way. She folded her hands in her lap. "Miss Darkin and I have plans for a comfortable *tête-à-tête*, and it will only bore you both."

What was she up to? "Do you enjoy fishing, Mr. Ward?" I asked in resignation, turning to the other man. "There is a pleasant spot near here that should afford us some good sport this time of year."

Ward's eyes flicked from one lady to the other. "I have been known to indulge in the activity now and again," he said with little enthusiasm. "It has been some time since I last enjoyed the sport. Lead on, Bywood."

With that, he and I were dismissed from the sitting room. We passed a maid carrying a tea tray as we made our way outside. I sent a footman off to retrieve the necessary equipment for the fishing venture. "Unless you would rather take yourself off to find some other amusement?" I asked, turning to my companion.

"Fishing isn't the worst way to pass a few hours," he said, still lacking any enthusiasm. "Though I daresay this will be the wrong time to catch anything worthwhile."

"You 're right," I agreed. "But what can we do? We were not wanted inside."

Ward nodded in agreement but said no more. The fishing gear was brought, and we started off on foot. "Your mother is aware you are courting Miss Ramsey?" Ward asked after several long minutes of unnerving silence.

Clearing my throat, I gave a quick nod. "I think everyone is aware of it by now. In fact, I believe I was the last one to find out about it."

He chuckled. "I see," he said, glancing around at the scenery. "I wondered if it was something like that. You could do a lot worse than Phoebe Ramsey, I suppose. I assume she comes with a good dowry and that's why your father made this arrangement?"

Father had mentioned money several times since I'd arrived. And he'd been irrationally annoyed when I had proclaimed I would pay the forfeit to the Ramseys. Was the Bywood family in need of funds?

"I could do a lot better," I commented.

"Better as in Miss Darkin? A pity you did not meet her earlier."

There was an odd note of teasing in his voice. "We're almost there," I said, gesturing to the stream ahead of us. Thankfully, Ward said no more on the subject because I had no intention of discussing the appeal of Miss Darkin with him or anyone.

As we drew nearer to the stream, I realized we wouldn't be alone. A man was crouching on the banks of the stream. He seemed to be looking for something, and when he glanced in my direction, I recognized him. I couldn't help but smile at the irony. "Mr. Lamotte," I said, feeling disappointed to be reencountering the man so soon. I had not thought of a plan to extract the ring from him, and he had left me with no doubts he did not desire to further our acquaintance. "Fancy meeting you on Bywood land."

"Well, if it isn't the young Mr. Bywood," Lamotte said, getting to his feet. "And Ward. This is a surprise. You've been away from London for most of the year. One might think you were hiding from something."

"Indeed," Ward said in the coldest tone of voice I had ever heard. "So this is where you vanished to when you are not cheating at cards. I will make sure to avoid the card tables while I am in the neighborhood."

At the obvious insult, Lamotte glared at Ward. Uneasy, I glanced between them. Just when I thought one of them would throw a punch, Lamotte gave a mocking bow and strode to where his horse was tied to a branch. He mounted and rode from the stream.

"If there was any chance of us catching anything, it's gone now. He is bound to have scared the fish away," I said, observing the muddied water. When I didn't get an answer, I shifted my gaze to my companion. Ward was staring moodily in the direction Lamotte had ridden in. "Is there a problem?"

"Lamotte is not someone I would refer to as 'good company.'" He sent a glance at the stream and snorted. "I will pass on the fishing this time. Perhaps another occasion will present itself. Good day, Bywood."

He spun on his heel and strode quickly away. Left on my own, I took a seat on a fallen log that had not yet been dealt with. Sighing, I rested my elbows on my knees and stared at the slowly moving water.

How curious Lamotte would be so set on maintaining his privacy, insisting on no one trespassing on what he viewed as his property, but happily traipsed over someone else's. And I couldn't rid myself of the idea that maybe he was the one behind the hole that caused my mother's accident.

"But why?" I said aloud. To make sure Miles didn't get the ring back? If the hole had been intended for Miles, as I suspected, why would Lamotte go to such lengths to hold onto a mere ring? "What is this all about?"

———◉———

I KEPT AWAY FROM THE house for as long as I could. My solitude did nothing to ease my troubled thoughts. In all honesty, my questions and suspicions only prompted more questions and doubts. If I wasn't careful, I would end up wary of every one of my acquaintance or a bit insane from trying to work it all out into some logical sense.

No one was in the sitting room when I poked my head through the doorway. In the hallway, I encountered George. "Was it your idea to have our mother leave her bed?" he demanded as soon as he saw me. He didn't give me the opportunity to answer as he continued, "It is just like you to concoct something idiotic like that. Do you realize the kind of damage you have done to her health?"

"What damage? Was Mama injured in some way?"

"She was so exhausted she went straight to her bed. She refused Rosamund's company!"

I barely kept from laughing. "Of course she did. Mama has been confined to her bed for months, so naturally, she would not have her strength as she used to. Once she gets back into the habit of being up, she will be more herself again."

"Since when did you study to be a physician?"

"I do not pretend to be a doctor, George. It's common sense," I said, shaking my head. "Why am I the only one who wants to help Mama improve? You want her to waste away in her bed?"

"Whether it does her some good or not, Father will be furious with you when he hears of this," George said, apparently abandoning the argument. "Maybe then you will learn to think before you act."

Scoffing, I stepped back. "When is he not furious with me over one thing or another? Besides, in this case, it was Mama's idea. She wanted to meet Miss Darkin, so she rose from her bed by her own choice. I had nothing to do with it."

Nevermind I had been the one to *suggest* the idea to her in the first place. George shook his head. "Luke, maybe Father wouldn't be furious with you if you listened to him for once," he said, putting his hand on my shoulder. "When you give him reason to be proud of you, he will be."

Immediately, I shrugged off his hand. "I have never given him a reason not to be proud of me."

"Oh, there you are." Rosamund's voice reached us. There was the rustle of silk as she walked up to link her arm with George's. "Lucas, we missed you at the competition this afternoon. I would have thought you would have enjoyed seeing your Phoebe excelling at archery. Knowing you were watching would have given her confidence, I am sure."

Meeting her gaze, I forced a smile, wanting to appear unconcerned. As expected, she raised her chin. "Thank you for your input, Rosamund. I'll keep that bit of advice in mind for the future. By the way, I crossed paths with your brother today."

Startled, she stared at me. "My brother? Wherever did that happen?"

"Down by the stream." I didn't miss the way her eyes widened. "If I had known he was such a sportsman, I would have invited him to join myself and Miles on our fishing excursions."

Rosamund twisted the ring on her right hand. "My brother is one who values his privacy," she said as Miles appeared at the far end of the hallway. He approached, looking wary and cautious. "I doubt he would have accepted the invitation."

"I don't believe that, since he has passed several evenings playing cards with Miles not so long ago," I said, nodding at my friend. "But if you will excuse me, Rosamund, I have letters to write, and I know Miles will want to give me an account of the archery competition."

Moving around them, I noticed the stunned expression on my friend's face. Rosamund gave an audible huff and pulled George off with her. "Is there something wrong, Miles?" I asked as I reached him. No one would have missed my tired, resigned tone as I spoke. Another problem was the last thing I needed.

"That ring," he said in bemusement. "That ring your sister-in-law had on her right hand. It's my ring; the one I gave Lamotte as security."

Chapter Twelve

The next day we at Bywood Hall joined the house party at the pond for an afternoon of outdoor activity. Blankets were spread out in the grass for the ladies. A rowboat had been dragged from somewhere and rested on the bank, waiting to be used.

I tried to keep my eyes on everyone tied up in the problems that had occupied my life, but doing so only gave me a headache. Phoebe stayed as far from me as she could get, and played a game of letters with Rosamund. This, of course, did nothing to help our effort to appear like a courting couple. Miles remained near the picnic baskets, chatting with Mrs. Williamson. Philippa was content to talk with her betrothed on a blanket, becoming animated as she did so.

By the pond, the Williamson girls began a game of Battledore and Shuttlecock, which had them laughing as soon as they started. Miss Darkin declined to join in, choosing instead to sketch in her book. Ward seemed bored with the whole afternoon, and the older members of the group were content to sit and chat about nothing in particular.

For a picnic, it was rather dull. No one seemed inclined to do anything remotely interesting. It was a pity, as I could recall many happy hours spent in that spot. My oldest sister, Jane, had taken every opportunity to explore the pond and the area around it. As I recalled, it was on a walk around the water that she agreed to marry Charles Castleton.

After an hour, I couldn't hide my yawn and Ward's expression betrayed that he was ready to find any excuse to take him away. The only thing keeping me at the site was the prospect of the meal. The Ramseys' cook made some of the best strawberry tarts and never failed to have them on hand for a picnic.

"Mr. Ward, we have heard precious little from you these past few days," Mrs. Ramsey said once we had all feasted on the meal provided and all other activities had slowed to nothing. "Surely you have some tale to entertain us this afternoon."

I was the only one close enough to hear the growl that sounded in Ward's throat. But when he faced the rest of the picnic members, there was a friendly smile playing on his lips. "Normally I am happy to comply, Mrs. Ramsey," he responded. "I fear, though, I have no new stories to amuse you with today."

"Well, then, you must tell everyone one of your old tales. The one about the highwayman is thrilling, and you tell it so well."

"Highwayman?" Rosamund repeated, sending a pointed look at me. "If Lucas is to be believed, there can be no harm from a highwayman."

As much as I wanted to argue the point, I settled for giving her a smile instead. It was enough to turn her expression sour. "Tell us, Ward," Mr. Williamson said eagerly. "I don't think I've ever heard of you being held up by a highwayman."

"Oh, I wasn't," Ward said with a smirk. "This took place not so long ago when I was invited to a house party similar to this one. The area, at the time, was being terrorized by a highwayman. All attempts to catch him or track him down were for naught. Many ladies, such as yourselves, lost their jewelry and men their money to this man."

He was a storyteller; there was no doubt about that. He had everyone leaning forward to hear what he would say next. Miss Darkin even closed her sketchbook to give him her full attention. I felt a twinge of jealousy at the fact.

"Tell them who it was, Ward!" Mrs. Ramsey said, her tone impatient. She glanced at everyone else. "You will not believe it when you hear it. I was astonished when I heard!"

Ward shook his head reprovingly. "Madame, allow me to tell this as it needs to be told. Fathers were forbidding their children, especially their daughters, from walking alone. This was the situation when I arrived. A groom had been injured when the occupants of a specific carriage refused to comply with the demands of the highwayman."

"Ward, you confirm what I told them all earlier this week," I said with a laugh. He directed a glare at me, unamused by my interruption to the tale he had been cajoled into telling. "Cooperation is the only way to go when a highwayman stops you on the road."

"Lucas, allow him to tell the story," George said sharply. "No one asked for your opinion."

"He is correct," Ward said to my surprise and before I could express my anger at my brother's words. "The gentleman who put up a fuss was a fool to think he would win out against someone desperate to steal. He was incredibly fortunate in the identity of the highwayman; otherwise, he could have been harmed. Possibly killed."

His words cast a slight shadow across the group. "One of the families that joined the house party was robbed no more than a mile from their ultimate destination, and after that day, there was a lull in the reports of his activity," Ward continued. "Until one day, a young lady and her siblings were walking from their home to join the house party for the afternoon activities."

"What happened, Mr. Ward?" Mrs. Williamson asked.

"These young people crossed the place the highwayman had last been," Ward said, continuing as though he had not been interrupted. "The two young men thought they spotted some tracks in the mud, and being the curious persons they are, they set off to follow those tracks. The younger of the ladies was impatient and followed after the two brothers, being of a more intrepid spirit than her sister, leaving the other young lady alone."

By this point, even I was intrigued by his tale. "When her siblings returned to the spot a mere two minutes later, they discovered their sister had been hit over the head," Ward said, raising his voice. "The highwayman had been in the area and had felt threatened."

Rosamund gave an audible gasp. "How dreadful." She clutched my brother's arm as Philippa squeaked in alarm.

"Oh, she made a quick and full recovery, Mrs. Bywood. Have no fear. Naturally, this caused even more alarm in the neighborhood. However, it did not last forever. The young lady who had been so cruelly attacked remembered what she had seen that had been a threat to the highwayman: a family ring. A young gentleman from the area couldn't bear to admit his debts to his father and had resorted to robbing his neighbors as the highwayman."

Exclamations rang out, and I frowned as I considered it. On the one hand, I could understand the feelings of the young man. I would have been reluctant to go to my own father had I incurred a great deal of debt from gambling or some foolishness but would I have resorted to robbing to avoid doing so?

"How did you come to know this all?" Mr. Talbot asked, raising his eyebrow. "I would hardly think this is the kind of story a family wants to be well known."

Ward shrugged his shoulders. "The young man was an acquaintance of mine. And Miss— the sister of the young lady attacked told me all when I pressed her for the information. I have, you noticed, kept quiet on the identity of these people. They all deserve to have their privacy respected, especially the young man who made such a terrible mistake."

"It is too bad of you even to tell it in the first place, Mr. Ward," Miss Darkin said, a note of righteous indignation in her voice. "Suppose the young man were to make a change in his behavior and come to regret his youthful actions? How will he feel if he returns to society only to hear everyone laughing about this story? Even if his name is not known, there is still the chance someone will put together the truth!"

"Olivia, none of us will go off and retell the story," Phoebe said. "It is meant to entertain. There's no need to take it so seriously."

When I glanced at Miles, I saw a strange, thoughtful look on his face and wondered what had caught his interest. "Well, I didn't mean to stir up a debate," Mrs. Ramsey said in agitation. "I thought it an amusing tale, no more."

"Lucas, you ought to take Phoebe out onto the pond," Rosamund said, getting my attention. "And we will speak no more on this subject."

"Well—" I struggled to find some valid excuse not to be trapped in a small boat with Phoebe Ramsey. If she intended on doing her best to avoid me, I would do so in return. I knew she wasn't fond of the water from all the times I had pushed her into the pond in retaliation for many things she had done to me first. "I don't think Phoebe enjoys—"

At the same time, Mrs. Ramsey said, "What a marvelous idea, Mrs. Bywood! You are an absolute genius. Phoebe, darling, would you like to go out in the rowboat?"

"Oh, of course," Phoebe said much to my surprise. "Olivia and I had talked yesterday about how much we wished to go out on the water. Olivia, put down your sketchbook and come along."

"Phoebe, my dear, the rowboat is not so big. Lucas will take you, and then I am sure Mr. Russell can take Miss Darkin afterward," Rosamund said, her tone persuading. "It is just the thing."

She was intent on arranging Miles and Miss Darkin as a match. Of everything she did that annoyed me, this particular thing needled me the most. "No, I know Lucas hates to be on the water," Phoebe said cheerfully. I blinked at her surprise. I didn't like the water? Since when? "Mr. Russell can take Olivia and me together. There is plenty of room for three."

Miss Darkin's eyebrows went up, but she set aside her book. She rose and allowed herself to be pulled to the rowboat. Miles followed them, a delighted expression replacing the calculating one. I caught Rosamund and George frowning in my direction, no doubt unhappy with my failure to comply with the scheme.

George apparently had forgotten the last time I had been on the pond with our neighbor; she had pushed me overboard because I tossed her doll into the water. I had been twelve, and I hadn't even wanted to be in the same boat with her. We had returned home wet, muddy, and furious with each other.

"Even if you hadn't told me your engagement was arranged, I would have guessed something was not quite right between you and Miss Ramsey," Ward said quietly when he moved to stand next to me. "You and she have to be the most ill-matched couple I've ever seen. I wish you great happiness in the future, Bywood, and hope you find a good mistress to liven up your days."

I leveled an unamused look in his direction, annoyed by the suggestion. It was generally accepted among those accustomed to Town standards that a man would have a mistress, especially if he were married. All that was expected was he be discreet about it, and his wife would turn a blind eye to the situation. The lady may even have her own discreet *affaire du cœur*.

However, I had every expectation I would find a wife I would want to be faithful to. Maybe that was a naive hope, but not one I was willing to abandon.

"Or perhaps you should find a way to get out of the engagement," Ward continued. "You already have the reputation of being unreliable. Use it to your advantage."

"That is a reputation I protest." That I already had a plan to break the engagement had nothing to do with the matter. "You may think how one is spoken of is of no consequence, but I do. I have done nothing to warrant these tales being told of me and I tire of hearing them."

A thoughtful expression crossed his face. "Unfortunately, since you have this reputation, there is nothing you can do to fight it off. It will cling to you forever. My advice is to embrace it. Stop caring about what others think of you."

Opening my mouth to object, I was interrupted by the sound of a loud splash and a simultaneous panicked cry from the pond. Twisting my head around, I spotted the rowboat, bottom side up and no sign of the occupants. Phoebe and my friend surfaced a moment later, Miles supporting the coughing and struggling girl.

"Good God!" Mr. Ramsey said as I scrambled to my feet. "Phoebe!"

Tearing off my jacket and waistcoat, I made quick work of untying my cravat and then bolted for the edge of the pond. I dove in and swam towards the overturned boat, where Miss Darkin had come up and clung to the boat. I passed Phoebe and Miles, who were not working well together in trying to make their way to the shore.

"Just relax, Miss Darkin," I said as I reached the boat. I put my arm around her waist. "I have you now."

"Indeed," she said in a breathless voice. She pushed the sagging brim of her hat away from her face, giving me a better view of her sparkling blue eyes. "You are prompt to rescue a lady, I see."

I pulled her to the safety of shore. Mr. Ward was up to his knees in the water. The ladies were ready with blankets, so I didn't have the opportunity to admire the sight of Miss Darkin in a wet, clinging dress. As I regained my breath, I told myself I was a gentleman and needed to focus on something more appropriate.

As Phoebe sobbed in her mother's arms, Mr. Ward asked Miss Darkin how the accident had occurred. She sent a sideways look at Phoebe but shook her head. "I am not sure," she said. "One minute all was well and the next we were in the water."

The accident brought the picnic to an end. As Phoebe and Miss Darkin were hurried to the carriages, Rosamund frowned at me. "I do hope neither of you expects to return with us. You're soaking wet and will quite ruin the fabric in the carriage."

"Not to worry, dear Rosamund," I said with a sigh. "Miles and I will walk."

A fitting end to an unenjoyable afternoon.

Chapter Thirteen

My life had become such a tangle. Since I had failed to untangle it myself, it was time to turn to the one place I could get help. Mama always knew what to do whenever I was concerned about something. I went to her room the day after the picnic, only to find Dr. Morgan was with her, a frown creasing his forehead.

"Is Mama well?" I asked worriedly, my mind immediately thinking the worst. "What's happened?"

"I'm afraid your mother has rather overdone herself, Master Lucas," he said. He wagged a finger at Mama as though she were a misbehaving child. "I must insist you remain in bed until I say it is safe for you to rise, Mrs. Bywood. You will do yourself no favors if you are up and about before you are ready. You may cause permanent harm."

"Surely some movement and fresh air would be better than none." I couldn't bear the thought that I was the cause of this downward turn. "It cannot be good for anyone to be in the same room for so long without a change."

Dr. Morgan, so familiar and yet aged at the same time, turned his frown on me. "I am the professional here, young man," he said sternly. "Trust me to know what is best for your mother. If she expects to recover her health even slightly, she will obey me this time."

"Luke just worries, Doctor," Mama said with a faint smile. "I shall be fine, dear. I fear I may have sat in a draft the other day. I feel weaker than before, nothing more."

"Then, you should have said something at the time." I went to her side. Her eyes scanned me, and her forehead began to wrinkle into a frown. "Miss Darkin would have understood, I'm sure. She will be distraught when she learns of this."

"Now don't you discuss my health with the neighbors, Luke Bywood. I do not need any more of that."

I raised my hand as though I were swearing to it. "I promise no one shall hear a word of it from me." What else could I do? She enjoyed her privacy as much as the next person and to know she must be talked of often must frustrate her. "Shall I leave you to get more rest now?"

"Not at all," Mama said even as the doctor said 'yes'. "Doctor, I must speak with my son. He would not seek me out unless he were in need of my advice. I'm sure no further harm will come to me from just a conversation."

How did she always know?

Heaving a sigh, Doctor Morgan gathered up his bag. He left after giving Mama strict instructions as to her health and informed me he intended on telling my father the same thing. I had little doubt I would be in a great deal of trouble once again from both Father and George when they learned I was responsible for Mama's new bout of ill health.

"Now, Luke, tell me all about the picnic," Mama said once we were alone. "I assume something happened that bothered you?"

"Hasn't Rosamund told you the story? I thought she or Philly would come straight to you."

She shook her head. "Rosamund has many duties to see to around the house," she said, an odd note of bitterness in her voice. "She barely ever comes to see me. It's better for us both that she does not. Philippa, as you know, is only concerned with her Mr. Talbot now he is in the area."

I chuckled and settled into the seat by her. It didn't take long to give a full account of the afternoon, ending with the accident at the pond. "Miles disappeared as soon as we returned. He joined us for dinner, but since then I haven't seen him. I have no idea what he intends to do now he knows where his ring is."

"His ring?"

Flinching, I shook my head. "It's a long story." I would at least keep Miles' secret. "I told him I would help him solve a problem, but now I don't know what he is thinking."

"Perhaps the strain of pretending to be something he is not is affecting him as much as it is affecting you. It cannot be easy to constantly hear the woman he loves is to marry you, even if he does know your courtship is a farce. To be perfectly honest, Luke, I think you might do better to end it now and allow all of you to continue with your separate lives."

With a sigh, I ran my hands through my hair. "Would that I could, Mama. It seems no matter what I do, someone will be disappointed in me."

"You concern yourself with others far too much, Luke." She coughed into her handkerchief before she continued. "You will do yourself harm if you continue with this play-acting."

"Mama, I don't see how it would be possible," I said with a forced laugh. "I know there will be hurt feelings on all sides when the Ramseys learn Phoebe will not marry me. Father says they have been depending on this connection. But as has been made clear to me, my reputation here isn't worth much anyway. I will be as I was before I arrived, no harm done."

Alarm filled Mama's face. "Your reputation? Not worth much? What do you mean?"

"Calm down, please," I said, catching her hand. "I simply refer to how I am not well thought of. I have been called a rapscallion, a scapegrace, and I don't know what else."

"A scapegrace? How—why would anyone call you that?"

Her outrage was palpable and made me smile. "Mama, they undoubtedly believe it because I am the rebel who went off on a Grand Tour despite disapproval from Father and you."

"But we never disapproved! Young men do so all the time. George may dislike traveling but why should you not get to see something of the world? Oh, this is outside of enough! What right has anyone to make such judgments about you? It is entirely uncalled for."

"Mama, please calm down," I said, concerned as she became more agitated. "You just said I ought not to concern myself with what people thought."

She focused a glare at me. "I will not calm down. You have done nothing to warrant these horrible names! And here I am stuck in this stupid bed with no way of putting those thoughtless people in their places."

I could well imagine how Mama would face the whole of the neighborhood and scold them all. Shaking my head, I squeezed her hands. "To be honest, the worst offenders are right in this house. You may call them up and set them straight whenever you wish to do so."

"Allow me to guess. George and his dear wife," Mama said with a scowl. "Well, you can be sure I will have words with them both as soon as I get some rest. They both should know better."

"I have no doubt you will put things right."

———◆———

AT DINNER, I KNEW MAMA had spoken to George because he avoided my gaze. I knew Rosamund had also been scolded because she glared at me and refused to speak to me for the entire meal. Mr. Talbot had been invited to join us, and when he happened to ask after Mama, George and Rosamund both had nothing to say, though Philippa had no qualms about detailing Mama's decline.

After dinner, two hours were spent playing a game of charades, which revealed a light-hearted side to Mr. Talbot I hadn't seen before. He even laughed on several occasions. As Philippa seemed to be much calmer than I ever remember her being before, I decided it would be a good match and gave them my silent, unasked for approval.

Miles did not make an appearance, and I assumed he had been invited to Lamridge for dinner. However, when I mentioned it, Mr. Talbot declined any knowledge of such an invitation being extended. Where was Miles and what was he up to?

Knowing his state of mind and his determination to get his family ring back, I had the feeling I should be worried.

The next morning, he appeared at the breakfast table and was more cheerful than he had ever been. That did not ease my mind. With George and Philippa at the table, I couldn't question him about his whereabouts. While we were eating and chatting, an invitation arrived for us all to dine at Lamridge that evening.

"How marvelous," Philippa said with delight. "I shall pen our acceptance immediately."

"Wait until Rosamund has agreed to go," George said to her, his tone reproving. "It would vex her if you accepted on her behalf without consulting her feelings on the matter."

I resisted the impulse to remark how we must always be considerate of others' feelings on matters. Unless, of course, it is about an arranged marriage. Then, the young man in question must be berated and forced to accept. However, I decided it would be best to remain silent. I'd made my feelings known on the matter.

"When you do respond, inform Mrs. Ramsey that while I will be unable to join them for dinner, I will be glad to join them for tea," Miles said casually.

Philippa stared at him in shock. "My goodness, Mr. Russell, you have been making yourself scarce these past few days," she said as she set aside the invitation. "Whatever have you been doing?"

Miles didn't even bat an eye at the question that verged on rude. "I have had business to settle, I'm afraid, Miss Philippa," he answered. "But I am certain it will be completed soon."

George got to his feet. "Speaking of business, this estate won't run itself. Luke, make yourself useful if you please. The Masons have been complaining about a leak in their roof. Stop in and see if it's all a hum, will you? They always did like you."

"Why don't we just send someone to fix it?" I asked, annoyed to be cast in the role of errand boy. "I have never known the Masons to make a complaint without basis."

My brother shook his head. "For once in your life, just do as I ask, Luke."

Crossing my arms, I stared at him. With a scowl, George left the room. "I wish you and George would get along," Philippa said softly. "You argue so much nowadays. It hardly makes things comfortable."

"I am afraid that is what happens when siblings grow up and form their own opinions of the world," Miles said philosophically. "I would be more concerned if they agreed on everything, especially on the points that result in Luke being used in an abominable way."

"Oh, that's not true at all! You make it sound as though Luke is mistreated." Philippa stood up, collecting the invitation. "I cannot speak to you both when you are in such impossible moods. I shall go 'consult' with Rosamund about whether we shall attend this dinner tonight or not."

She swept from the room, and I burst out in laughter. "I thank you for your defense, Miles."

"I realized we all have been treating you terribly, and it is not fair to you," he said humbly. "You won't have me imposing on your good nature anymore, Luke. I have this matter of my ring in hand, and I expect to be in a position to propose to Phoebe by the end of the week."

I eyed him suspiciously. "Just what are you up to? How do you intend to get your ring from Rosamund? I hardly think she is the kind of woman to give it up on your word, and her brother has already proven he has no intention of being agreeable."

As he rose from his seat, Miles shook his head and chuckled. "As I said, I have it in hand." Hearing it a second time did not leave me anymore reassured. "I will see you later this evening, Luke."

He left the room, and I was alone. In the quiet, I contemplated what he could be up to as I finished my coffee. "I have no idea," I said aloud. Shaking my head, I went off to the stable to take Phaeton for a ride.

THOUGH I'D HAD NO INTENTION of allowing my brother to order me around, I found myself going past the Masons' cottage. As always, Mrs. Mason was delighted to see me and sat me down in her kitchen for some tea and biscuits. She gathered the children around the table, and they all listened with interest as I explained where I had been and the things I had seen. The middle son had a hundred questions about my trip.

Once a full hour had been spent in that manner, Mrs. Mason showed me the roof. A recent storm had caused some damage, and with the latest rain, they had noticed the leak that had developed. "I wouldn't be asking," she admitted, "but it leaks right over the children."

I assured her it would be no trouble at all to have it fixed. As soon as I left the cottage, I rode Phaeton to the thatchers and directed him to repair the Masons' roof sooner rather than later. The Mason family had lived on and worked our land for three generations, and I would not see any of them becoming ill over a leaky roof.

As I set off across the countryside, I breathed in the clean air. Though Miles' certainty that he would be reclaiming his ring was concerning, I couldn't help but be relieved the failing pretense of Phoebe and I being involved in a courtship would come to an end. With the mystery behind Mama's accident mostly solved, I would be free to chart my own course once again. What would I do first?

Miss Darkin's face rose up in my mind, laughing in spite of being thoroughly soaked.

"Maybe," I said to myself. Maybe she would be a part of my future.

A curious sight caught my attention then, driving away the idea of a possible romance. Mr. Ward and Mr. Lamotte were in the middle of a field standing practically nose to nose. Given the cold greetings they had exchanged before, this could not have been a good thing. As I rode towards them, debating whether to get involved or not, Lamotte brought his fist up and planted a solid facer. Ward reeled several steps back but remained on his feet.

Lamotte moved as though he was going to strike again with Ward not even looking up. "Enough!" I shouted as firmly as possible. I reined Phaeton in by them and slid to the ground. "What is this about?"

With a sneer, Lamotte took a step back. "Mind your own business, Bywood. This is a gentlemen's dispute between Ward and myself. I wouldn't expect you to know anything about it."

"Given that you are on Bywood land, I have the right to make it my business, Mr. Lamotte," I snapped at him. "And you would do well to cease implying insults, sir. I may be easygoing in general, but you will find my patience only goes so far."

My threat drew another sneer, but Lamotte continued his retreat. Ward straightened and said, "I'm serious, Lamotte. I cannot wait much longer."

"You will wait until I am ready," Lamotte said sharply.

Ward stepped forward, his hands curling into fists. "Leave it," I said, stepping in front of him. "Mr. Lamotte, you do not wish us on your land. Now I request you to stay off of ours. Good day."

Scowling, Lamotte spun on his heel and stalked away. "You have done yourself no favors by taking my side, Bywood," Ward said. "You should have kept on riding and allowed me to settle it my way. This has nothing to do with you."

"I am not one to see a friend threatened and just ride past. What was that about?"

He leveled an incredulous look at me. "How can you ask me that?" He ran the back of his hand over his mouth, wiping away the trickle of blood. "A gentleman never reveals the nature of his debts."

I chuckled as I connected the dots. "Lamotte owes you money. And it is a great deal, I am assuming?" Ward glared at me. "Well, to be fair, he is waiting to be repaid himself for a debt. He may not be in a position to pay you."

Mentally, I began to put more of the pieces together. Rosamund had the ring now. Why had Lamotte given away the ring he would have to get back to get the money from Miles? Though the fact he didn't have the ring explained why he kept putting Miles off about repaying.

"Oh, what a mess," I said with a sigh.

Ward raised his eyebrow, once again the haughty gentleman. "You would be better served to break off your engagement with Phoebe Ramsey and return abroad, Bywood. Leave everyone to manage their own affairs."

"I know it, but I am committed to the course I am on," I said with regret. I paused and chuckled. "I do hope it will be resolved before I am dragged to Bedlam Asylum."

He shook his head at my attempt at being witty. "So, if your friend must repay Lamotte, he is the one I must press," he said, returning to the topic at hand. I blinked in surprise. "Did you think you were the only one clever enough to put two and two together?"

"Well, as Lamotte is not in a position to accept payment and return the security Miles gave him, I don't think pressing my friend will do any good."

Shaking his head, Ward scowled. "I cannot wait much longer. It has been long enough as it is."

"Are you so pressed for funds?"

"You are impertinent."

Unaffected, I shrugged my shoulders. "I can assure you the end of the Ramseys house party will set many things in motion." Turning, I mounted Phaeton. "I look forward to our race tomorrow, Mr. Ward."

A resigned expression on his face, he nodded. Nudging Phaeton's sides, I rode away from him. "That is the last time I try to do the honorable thing." I almost meant it. "It only complicates things."

Chapter Fourteen

When I returned from my ride late that afternoon, two things occurred. Butler informed me that Father wished to speak to me. At the same time, he presented me with a letter. Pocketing my letter to read later, I went to Father's office.

George was also there, and he seethed quietly in the corner. He had learned about my arrangements for the repair of the Masons' roof, and Father's nod of approval only compounded his anger. "Well done, Lucas. It is better for something to be done before it is too late. There may be hope for you yet."

The complement left me feeling hollow, and I didn't have anything else to say on the subject. "How is Mama today?" I asked, bracing myself for a scolding about being responsible for her relapse. "She was sleeping when I looked in on her earlier."

Once again, Father surprised me. "She seemed a bit improved," he said, sounding genuinely pleased. "Philippa took up flowers for her and brightened the room. You know how women are about those things."

George still had his arms crossed and a grim expression on his face. It seemed it would take some time for him to cease being irritated that I had acted without his permission. I tapped the desk to attract his attention. "Will you and Rosamund be joining us to dine with the Ramseys tonight?"

Immediately, George sent an anxious glance at the clock. "Oh, yes. In fact, we should all get ready to go. Rosamund will have our heads if we are late."

"You boys enjoy yourselves tonight," Father said with a fond smile. "Philippa has already sent my regrets as I believe an evening with your mother is in order. Every moment I can spend with her is important now. George, you make sure Lucas behaves himself."

"I do not need a nursemaid!" I exclaimed.

At the same time, George said, "I'm not sure anyone is up to such a weighty responsibility. He's never listened to me before and I don't think he's about to start now. Luke will do what he wants when he wants no matter what anyone says."

There would have been no use in denying it, and I held my tongue. I walked out of the office ahead of him. No matter what he said, I knew I had done what was best for the estate and for one brief moment I had my father's approval. As far as I was concerned, it had been a good day.

Taking the steps two at a time, I headed up upstairs. I could hear Philippa chatting away with her maid in her room as I went past and it made me smile. The oak door that stood at the threshold of Rosamund's room did not block the sound of my sister-in-law's raised voice. Flinching, I quickened my steps until I was well away and felt sorry for whoever was unfortunate enough to be my sister-in-law's maid.

Knowing I would not need hours to get ready for dinner, I settled into a chair in my room and opened my letter.

I WAS IN THE MIDDLE of tying my cravat when there was a loud knock on my door. "Yes?" I said, keeping my eyes on my mirror. The door opened, and Philippa stuck her head in. "What's wrong, Philly? Am I keeping Rosamund waiting?"

"As a matter of face, you are," my sister said, rolling her eyes. "She insists she has important things to discuss with Mrs. Ramsey and the Williamson girls. Are you ready now or do you want us to go ahead?"

For a moment, I considered. I refused to let Rosamund put me on a timetable that regularly changed and only she was in charge of. "I think I would prefer to walk over. Express my sincerest regrets to her, if you please."

"I will not lie for you, Luke. Just make sure you're not late. There's nothing a girl hates more than her beau being late."

It seemed ridiculous that to be late was what a girl would hate the most. I could think of at least half a dozen different actions that would be worse. I just laughed at Philippa as she closed the door, leaving me to finish dressing.

Ten minutes later, I was satisfied with my appearance. I made my way down to the hall where Butler had my hat and cane waiting. "Don't wait up for me, Butler," I said cheerfully. "I might be out late."

"This is not London or any other foreign city, Master Lucas," he said with a disapproving stare. "I do hope you will return at a decent hour."

Chuckling, I donned my hat and caught the sleek cane in my hand. "Perhaps, but you never know what kind of adventure one will have while walking. Has Mr. Russell returned from his business?"

"Mr. Russell has not."

It still puzzled me what Miles was up to, but if it brought an end to my 'courtship,' then I was happy to allow him the freedom to do as he wished without any questioning from me. At least, not *much* questioning. I only hoped it didn't create any more of a tangle in my affairs.

If it did, I would be tempted to wash my hands of it all, break the engagement, and leave them all to sort it out without my help.

In the interest of keeping Phaeton rested before the upcoming race, I set out on foot. An evening walk wasn't what I had been planning on, but I was willing to make do. It wasn't far, even if I did take the road instead of cutting across the property. I knew the evening dew would do irreparable harm to my breeches.

There was a different kind of peace when walking in the twilight. Few birds were awake to chirp and sing their songs. Owls hooted, and small animals stirred the grass alongside the road. There wasn't a soul to be seen as I walked.

I had never honestly considered myself to be someone who enjoyed solitude, but since I had come back home, maybe the description was more accurate than anything else. I enjoyed the company of friends, and I would never turn down the opportunity of having a good time. At the same time, there did come the point when quiet was all I needed.

The crack of a gunshot destroyed the peaceful nature of the evening, and I came to a halt, listening carefully. Poachers weren't uncommon in our area, and for the most part, we overlooked them. But the shot had come from close by, too close for my comfort.

There wasn't a second shot, but I did hear shouting. I hesitated for a moment and then plunged into the sparse woods to my right. As cautiously as I could, I moved towards the sound. I knew the trees would only provide minimal cover, but I was not idiot enough to go charging into a situation that involved guns.

Before I got near enough to have a clear view, someone came crashing through the trees. "Come back here, villain!" I recognized George's voice. What had happened?

The man tripped on a stone and hit the ground. "Blast it!" he said as he struggled to his feet.

"Miles?" I asked incredulously. He had something wrapped around the lower half of his face and was dressed in questionable apparel. "What are you doing? What happened?"

He spun towards me and swore. "Luke, we have to get out of here." Charging forward, he grabbed my arm and jerked me around. "Come on! If we're spotted, everything will be ruined!"

George? I wanted to ask what Miles had done but chose instead to follow him. I heard the snap of twigs underfoot as my brother drew nearer. "Your accomplice won't help you, ruffian!" George shouted furiously. "Stop or I'll shoot!"

The loud crack of a pistol shot echoed through the trees and then liquid fire burned across my upper right shoulder. Crying out, I staggered, nearly going down on my knees. It took me a moment to realize what had just happened.

My brother had shot me.

Miles tightened his grip on my other arm and pulled me along. I focused on my breathing and tried not to think of the pain that ran from my shoulder down to my fingers. My friend angled us towards the road, got us across, and threw me down to the ground. He stretched out beside me and waited.

It felt as though an eternity passed until the sound of pursuit faded. Miles lifted his head and glanced around. "I think we lost him."

I reached over and grabbed his arm. "Miles, I hope you know this could put a damper on our friendship," I said through gritted teeth. It felt only fair to warn him that I was not pleased about any of this.

"Stop being dramatic," he said, trying to pry my fingers off. "I thought you would be happy, Luke. I got the ring."

"Do you mean to tell me you just stole a ring from my sister-in-law?" I asked, my voice rising in anger and pain. Something warm was running down my injured arm, and I knew it was blood. "Miles, how stupid are you? You just committed a crime!"

He managed to escape my grip and pulled out of my reach. "Luke, it's fine. I will tell Phoebe she will be unable to wear the ring until after we are married and then we will not be here. No one will ever know. It was my ring in the first place. I was just taking it back."

A disbelieving laugh left my lips, though amusement was the furthest thing from my mind. "You underestimate my sister-in-law. You will cross paths at some point, and I know Rosamund will remember that ring and how she lost it."

Shaking his head, Miles stood up and glanced around. "Come on. We need to get changed and get to Lamridge before anyone connects us to this. Why are you still on the ground? Luke, we need to move."

"Miles, I was shot!"

In the fading light, he stared down at me. "I'm sure it cannot be as bad as that." He reached down to help me up. "Your brother wasn't even aiming at us. He'd never actually shoot a person."

Ignoring his hand, I struggled up. A wave of nausea and dizziness hit. As I stumbled, Miles grabbed me by the shoulders, and I couldn't keep from yelping in pain. "Luke, are you well?" he asked in concern.

"No, I told you I was shot!"

With my equilibrium restored, I brushed him off and started walking. I dearly wanted a drink. "Why didn't you tell me you were planning something like this?" I asked. The pain made me more snappish than usual, but I felt I had the right to be. "I could have told you it was an idiotic idea."

"Well, I knew you would have some objection," Miles said as he fell into step beside me. "How bad is your arm?"

"It's certainly not good."

"I have Skriven waiting for me at the hall. I am certain he will be able to bandage you up. I hardly think summoning a physician would be a good thing."

Even though Miles wouldn't see me, I rolled my eyes. George wouldn't know whether his shot had hit one of the 'highwaymen' or not, but he would undoubtedly warn Dr. Morgan to be on the lookout for a wounded man. As much as I hated it, I would have to keep this a secret, just like everything else I was carrying.

———————◦———————

BY THE TIME THE HALL was in view, my fingers felt sticky with my blood. Miles came up on my left side and supported me, not saying a word. He steered me towards the servants' entrance, where the door was open. We had just stepped across the threshold, and the tall, taciturn Skriven was on my other side.

"I assume there was trouble, Mr. Russell?" he asked.

"Mr. Bywood has had an unfortunate accident," Miles said, making it sound like the whole thing was my fault. I muttered my annoyance, but he ignored me. "We, of course, would like to keep this incident quiet."

"Of course, sir. I will gather what I need and meet you in Mr. Bywood's room."

Nodding, Miles pushed me down the narrow hallway to the equally narrow staircase. "If you could pick up your feet a little more, it would be beneficial," he said as I stumbled on the first step. "We don't have much time to get from here to Lamridge before everyone begins to be suspicious."

"I'm sorry for being so disobliging, Miles," I said, unable to rein in my sarcasm. "I shall endeavor to make sure that the next time I get shot while trying to assist you, I do not have any pressing engagements."

My friend scowled at me, but thankfully stopped talking. We managed to make it all the way up to the correct area of the house. It was with relief I was finally able to sit down in my room. Nothing had changed in the half hour I was gone.

A glass was put into my hand. "Drink that," Miles said as he pulled on my jacket. "You look like you could use it."

Shrugging my uninjured shoulder, I swallowed the brandy in one go. It burned going down and sent a warm feeling through me. I leaned forward so Miles could pull my jacket off me. He quickly stripped me of all my clothes from the waist up.

"These can never be used again," he said, tossing my shirt and jacket into the fireplace.

The flames that had been dying down flared up as my clothes caught on fire. I wouldn't miss them, but I did feel a twinge of guilt at the waste. I hissed in pain and jerked away when my friend poked at my wound. "I'm going to need another drink if you're going to do more of that," I said, holding the empty glass out to him.

Miles took the glass from my hand. "Not too much, though." Skriven entered with a fresh bowl of water. "Your brother would be suspicious if you were to be a trifle disguised given he left you sober and it would be offensive to the Ramseys."

"As if George has never seen me drunk before." Twisting my head, I shifted my attention to the wound. The sight of the blood oozing from the crease in my shoulder made my stomach clench, and I had to look away. "You do remember he gave us both brandies for the first time, don't you?"

As the valet began cleaning my arm, which made me even more queasy, Miles chuckled. "I remember being sick the next morning. And your mother made us spend the morning with her, and we tried so hard not to be sick in front of her."

The memory made me smile, but my mirth vanished as a needle pierced my skin. With a yelp of pain, I dared to glance over. "My apologies, sir," Skriven said, insincerely. "But needs must."

Swallowing hard, I leaned my head back and stared up at the ceiling. "You may have the ring now, but it doesn't change anything else," I said, focusing on our dilemma. "You still have to repay the debt to Lamotte, and he's going to refuse to take the payment because he cannot give you the ring."

"Why are you concerned about that?" Miles asked, waving his hand. "Now I can propose to Phoebe with a clear conscience. All will be as it should be."

His logic made my head spin. He still had a debt to repay, and couldn't know that Lamotte needed that money to compensate Ward, who needed the funds. I sighed and tried not to flinch away from the needlework Skriven was doing on my arm. "I will be sure to praise the advantages of living in foreign lands when I am at supper tonight," I said. "Phoebe will be free to receive your addresses soon."

"So you haven't changed your mind about that."

Surprised, I lifted my head to look at him. He was steadfastly avoiding my gaze, choosing instead to stare at my window. "Why would I have changed my mind? I gave you my word. I have no desire to marry Phoebe, and despite what everyone seems to think of me, I am a man who keeps his word."

My friend cleared his throat. "Of course," he said quickly.

"I assure you the time I have spent with Phoebe Ramsey has not changed my opinion of her." If anything, I was even more convinced she was a hen-witted girl and had no hope she would ever overcome it.

"What do you mean by that?"

"Never mind."

Miles' glare said he did mind it. "Sometimes I don't understand you, Luke," he said, leaning against the bedpost. "You've been rude since you got back from your trip. Is that what travel does to a person?"

"I hardly think anything I've said can be construed as rude." Well, maybe one or two things. Clearing my throat, I shook my head. There was a painful tug on my arm, and I glanced over to find Skriven tying off the thread. "You have an unusual skill set, if I may say so, Skriven."

The valet gave a slight smile. "Perhaps," he said. He wound a pristine length of neckcloth around the stitched wound. "Will that be all, Mr. Bywood, or will you need my services in dressing for the dinner party?"

I considered the effort it would take to dress without causing further injury to myself. "If it's not too much trouble, I would appreciate the assistance." I could hardly believe I said those words after my determination to be independent of such help.

With a nod, Skriven hurried to dispose of the materials he had used and then went to my wardrobe. "You'll be coming with me for dinner," I said to Miles as the valet pulled a fresh shirt and jacket out.

"I refuse to throw off Mrs. Ramsey's table arrangements," Miles said immediately. "They do not expect me until after the meal."

"Well, I'm sure Mrs. Ramsey would understand I met you on my way here, we stopped to exchange news, and I convinced you to have a meal with everyone else, instead of the mediocre offerings at the inn. It will explain why we arrived later and so we will, hopefully, avoid being suspected as highwaymen."

Grimacing, Miles considered it as Skriven helped me to dress. "I suppose it would be good to see Phoebe," my friend said thoughtfully as the valet tied my neckcloth into a

Mathematical knot. "I have not had a chance to speak to her in a few days. I can assure her that all has been made right."

"There you go." I glanced at the mirror and grimaced. My face was paler than usual, no doubt from the blood loss. "Miles, at least allow me one last drink to fortify myself for the walk to Lamridge ."

Miles poured a measure of brandy for himself and me. We both drank and then Miles led the way to the back staircase. I determined that, somehow, I would make it to the Ramsey's house and get through the dinner party.

How had my life come to this?

Chapter Fifteen

Exhaustion hung on me as Miles and I approached Lamridge . All I wished was to crawl into my bed and remain there for a day or two. There was a group of servants outside the house. Some had guns in hand, and others were carrying lanterns. They appeared to be preparing to do a search.

I kept from glancing at Miles as we kept our distance. The butler allowed us into the house and then showed us to the drawing room. It seemed everyone in the room was talking at the same time. Beside me, Miles appeared taken aback as Phoebe wailed something undecipherable and clung to her mother's arm. Rosamund was seated in the center of the room, waving her fan in front of her face.

"Has something happened?" I asked, raising my voice to be heard over everyone. "I saw the servants making preparations to make a search of some kind."

"Lucas! Where have you been?" George demanded, spinning around. "Rosamund and I were held up on the road by highwaymen. I managed to hit one of them so they couldn't have gone far."

"A highwayman? Here?" Miles responded, his tone shocked. A little too shocked if I were to be perfectly honest. There was such a thing as overdoing a matter, and I could only be glad that everyone else was in such a frantic state that they didn't notice the dramatic tone of his voice. "Don't be ridiculous, Bywood. What would entice a highwayman to come here?"

"It's true!" Rosamund exclaimed, her voice a shrill screech that made me flinch. She held her right hand out. "They took my ring. The awful man pulled it right from my finger like an absolute brute!"

Ward was watching me in a disconcertingly keen way. "Did you not hear anything or see anyone on your walk here?" he asked. "There has been a great deal of shouting and screaming."

"I came by way of the pond," I said. I would have shrugged, however, to do so would only cause myself pain. "I ran into Miles there and persuaded him to join us for dinner. We saw no one."

"Well, there was that shadow," Miles corrected.

Taken aback, I swung my head to stare at him. What was he doing? "You imagined things, Miles," I sdaid firmly. "I didn't see anything."

"Where was this shadow?" Mr. Ramsey asked. "I am sending all of our male servants out to search for these villains. If there is a place to start, it will be all the better for us."

"It was just this side of the pond," Miles responded eagerly. I shifted my foot enough to knock his ankle. He cleared his throat. "Of course, as Luke said, it was just a shadow. I thought perhaps it was a poacher, but Luke said not to worry about it."

George stiffened. "Lucas! You know we do not encourage poaching."

"Poaching happens, George," I said defensively. "What do you expect me to have done? Run after him and demand he stop? How ridiculous that would have been!"

"You wouldn't say it was ridiculous if it was your estate or your animals being stolen.."

Mr. Ramsey cleared his throat. "I believe we are getting away from the point here," he said, calmly. "Of course I understand your concerns about poaching, George. It is a very serious matter. Very serious! After we eat, I will join the search. I know my own lands better than anyone, save my steward. If there is someone hiding out there, I will find him."

"Mr. Bywood, you're looking a bit faint," Ward remarked. "Never say the walk from Bywood Hall to here has left you winded."

"It has not," I said sharper than I had meant. Why was he so observant? Did he suspect something? I dared to glance at him from the corner of my eye. The tall man had an infuriatingly smug expression on his face.

"Why must we speak about Lucas?" Rosamund demanded, closing her fan with a snap. Clearly, she didn't appreciate losing the attention of everyone in the room just as I didn't appreciate gaining the same attention. "He was not accosted by villains! My nerves have been shattered by this whole thing."

"We should go in to dinner," Mrs. Ramsey said desperately. This would be the second time that the poor woman's plans were cast awry by unfortunate events. Miss Darkin and Phoebe's plunge into the pond had put a sudden end to the picnic, and now the attack of a 'highwayman' was threatening to ruin her dinner party.

The suggestion managed to calm everyone, and each moved to go into the dining room. Miles hurried to take Phoebe's arm, no doubt to have a moment to inform her that she would soon be free of me as a beau. I paused for a moment to take a deep breath and close my eyes. How was I going to get through this evening?.

Once this whole thing was over, I was going to be in pressing need of a holiday.

"Mr. Ward is correct, Mr. Bywood. You don't look well at all."

With a start, I opened my eyes to see that Miss Darkin was by me. When had she approached? "A fine welcome that is," I said in as light and careless a manner as I could manage. Extending my arm, and trying not to wince as I did so, I asked, "May I escort you in, Miss Darkin?"

Her blue eyes scanned my face, and she shook her head, disappointment written across her face. "If you're not going to tell me the truth," she said with a sigh. She looped her arm with mine. "I believed you and I were becoming friends, Mr. Bywood."

Blast! I had warned Miles that confiding the truth to Phoebe would be a bad idea. I knew the honorable thing would be to follow my own advice and not tell Miss Darkin, even though I knew she would keep the secret. She was as much a part of this as anyone.

Trying to decide what to do, I led her to the dining room. "I'm sorry," was all I said before I was seating her next to Miles. I moved to my assigned seat between Phoebe and Mrs. Darkin.

Chatter around the dinner table centered on the highwayman as I knew it would. Using my right hand to eat without showing pain required all of my focus. My shoulder burned more and more with each course that was brought to the table. Thankfully, Phoebe was ignoring me, and Mrs.

Darkin was content to direct her conversation to George, who was on her left.

It was with relief that I saw the ladies leave the table. I collapsed into my seat as soon as the door shut. Ward shifted in his chair so that he was facing me. "I know many who dislike being social, but none of them have ever appeared so strained, Bywood," he said as he accepted a glass of port. "Is a dinner so difficult for you to endure?"

I took my own glass in my left hand. "Some evenings are harder than others, Mr. Ward," I said. Across the table, Miles was watching us with concern.

Ward made a slight humming sound as if he did not believe me. "Are you keeping Phaeton in fine condition for our race? I don't want there to be any excuses or complaints when I trounce you."

The race. I had completely forgotten that I was expected to race Phaeton against his Tesoro in a mere two days. "Naturally," I answered automatically. How was I going to manage a race without revealing my injury or doing myself further damage? "I do expect to give you a run for your money, Mr. Ward. What's more I expect I will be doing the trouncing."

His expression became one of amusement. "It's strange, isn't it? Just a few days after I tell the story of a young man of a respectable family acting as a highwayman to pay his debts, a highwayman randomly chooses this neighborhood to rob?" he asked, changing the subject completely. "It's almost as if my tale had inspired someone."

Sipping the port to buy myself some time, I mentally cursed Miles' impetuous actions that had led us to this situation. Ward was intelligent enough to have made the connection. Who else would come to the same conclusion?

"Do you take credit for inspiring a man to criminal actions?" I asked, trying to think of some way to avoid continuing the conversation without arousing further suspicion. "I'm not sure I would be proud of such a thing."

Before Ward could say another word, Mr. Ramsey was rising to his feet. "If you will excuse us, gentlemen," he said. "George and I must join the search for this highwayman. Please, join the ladies and keep them from being overly concerned."

"Surely, we could be of use," Ward said, though he did not seem enthused about the idea. "Many hands make the load light, and all that."

"I can show you where I saw the shadow," Miles volunteered eagerly, pushing himself up.

"I thank you for your generous offers, but I don't feel we should leave the ladies unguarded," Mr. Ramsey told them. I held back a sigh of relief. "Taking Lucas away from his betrothed tonight would be unthinkable. Phoebe would never forgive me. After all, he has hardly seen her more than a few moments at a time this past week."

"I suspect you and Miles would only get in the way," George said to me as he passed by. He kept his voice low. "Be so good as to escort Rosamund home. Try not to offend her too much. She has had a difficult evening."

Had I felt up to it, I would have made a face at him and made some witty remark. Instead, I lifted my left shoulder in as much of a shrug as I could manage.

"I will walk out with you gentlemen," Mr. Talbot offered, getting hastily to his feet.

I suspected that he disliked Miles and myself, and wanted to keep as much distance between us as possible. The door closed behind the three men, and Ward glanced between myself and Miles. "Now that the ears that should not hear are gone, why don't you two tell me what you were truly up to."

There was a part of me that believed telling Ward could be the right course of action. He, I was sure, would not rush off to tell my brother or Mr. Ramsey, as Phoebe undoubtedly would. Maybe he would even think of a way for us to escape this situation Miles had landed us in.

"I don't know what you mean." Miles drained his glass and set it down. "The ladies will be expecting us. We should go to them."

Ward shook his head. "If you are that eager to be bored out of your skull, then by all means, let us go," he said, lapsing back into his reserved, cold demeanor. I couldn't help but feel I had missed an opportunity.

———◆———

AS I WALKED INTO THE drawing room, I was fully aware of how much was depending on me making a good performance. Of course, the scene was missing a few key players. With Mr. Ramsey not present, I would have to be so convincing to Mrs. Ramsey that her husband would have no choice but to accept a break between Phoebe and myself.

Faced with the group I had to convince, I took a deep breath. All those times I had play acted with my older sisters were finally proving useful. At least I would not have George present to argue with me.

"I have fortuitous news," I announced cheerfully. "I have heard from my friend in Italy. He knows of the perfect cottage for me to purchase."

There was a gasp, and I couldn't be sure who it came from. I beamed at the group, inviting them to share my pleasure. "He what?" Phoebe asked, clearly not comprehending that it was time for our 'courtship' to end. "I don't understand. What cottage?"

"What news is this?" Rosamund demanded as I had expected.

"Oh, of course! You did say you are planning on living abroad, Mr. Bywood, did you not?" Miss Darkin said. Clever lady that she was, she'd realized what I was doing and was assisting as she could. And I had thought she was angry with me. "I have heard the Italian countryside is beautiful."

I nodded acknowledgment, barely sparing a glance in her direction. I kept my focus on those I needed to convince. "The society there surpasses London, I would wager. I shall be content there when I am not traveling elsewhere."

"A cottage in Italy?" Mrs. Ramsey exclaimed. "What can you be thinking?"

"I think it would be economical. I had considered Italy or even Greece before I decided that country would be far too extravagant."

Phoebe's eyes had widened. "M-Mr. Bywood," she stammered. "I know you mean this as a jest, knowing how my dear mother will react, but I beg you will cease this at once.

You might be amusing yourself, but the rest of us are hardly mirthful."

For a moment, I stared at her. She couldn't be so hen-witted she could not see what I was doing.

"I do remember you mentioning this venture before, Mr. Bywood," Miss Darkin spoke up, coming to my rescue once again. "How exciting for you! I have often wondered what life would be like outside of our own country. Phoebe, you must promise me that you will write to me often and tell us all everything you do."

Pulling her hand from my grasp, Phoebe spun to face Miss Darkin with an astonished expression on her face. "Lucas is not serious, Olivia," she said, her tone chiding. "Please do not encourage him in this fanciful notion."

"You may ask anyone, Miss Ramsey," I said, struggling to keep up the cheerfulness. I wanted to smack her until she came to her senses. Or what amounted to sense with Phoebe Ramsey. "I received a letter today. This is no passing fancy."

At least that point wasn't fanciful. In reality, the letter had contained an invitation to return to Italy, so technically I didn't feel I was lying. That probably would not save me from Mother when she heard about this, though.

"What he said is true," Rosamund said reluctantly. Everyone had focused on her to confirm my words. "He spoke to George about it earlier."

As it happened, I hadn't mentioned the letter to my brother at all. My suspicions that she had been prying into my correspondence was correct. "There, you see?" I said, putting this information aside to deal with later. "I expect he will send a sketch of the place soon and I can begin making plans."

Phoebe stared at me, and I saw her eyes light up. "I-I suppose there could be some sense in what you say, Lucas," she said, dashing my hope that she had caught on at last. "There are advantages to living in another country, I suppose. A young lady could purchase a new wardrobe that cannot compare to others."

The delight in her voice grew with every word. As she stepped closer, Miss Darkin's expression became one of alarm. "Well, of course," I said, trying to think quickly. "But a new wardrobe will have to be sturdy clothing, you understand. All of our wealth will go into traveling. There will hardly be a need for a new gown once we are wed."

Horror appeared on Phoebe's face as she took this information in. "No new gown?" she echoed faintly. "Travelling?"

"You can hardly expect us to live in a country and not take advantage of the views and art there!"

"You are a beast, Lucas!" Rosamund exclaimed. There was a fury in her eyes when I glanced her way. "Have you no consideration for others? Miss Ramsey deserves all the new gowns she wishes for! And she shouldn't be forced to sacrifice anything! Views? Art?"

"Why, Mrs. Bywood, I would have expected a lady like you to understand," Miss Darkin said, coming fiercely to my defense. "Everything Mr. Bywood has said makes perfect sense and is reasonable."

"Shall we play whist?" I asked, changing the subject. "I would like the opportunity to win back what I lost from Ward."

Ward, who had been looking on with amusement, raised an eyebrow. After a moment, he nodded. "I suppose that is the

decent thing to do." Relief surged through me. He definitely
deserved an explanation at the end of this. "After all you will
need that hundred pounds for your traveling and the upkeep of
a wife."

Mrs. Ramsey waved her fan frantically in front of her face.
Philippa was staring at me as though I had grown a second head
and Mr. Talbot scowled in disapproval. Miles, oddly enough,
was glowering at me, his expression matching Rosamund's.
Mrs. Darkin simply appeared confused by the whole thing.

"What an excellent friend you are, Mr. Ward," Miss Darkin
exclaimed.

I could not have agreed with her more. Strange that
between the person I thought was my best friend and someone
I had known for a matter of weeks, it would be the stranger that
was behaving as a friend ought. "Miss Ramsey, why don't you
play us something pleasant?" I suggested. "Mr. Talbot, will you
join us? Miles?"

The hostess should have been the one suggesting activities
for us, but Mrs. Ramsey seemed to be in a state of shock. No
other lady was acting on her behalf. "I will turn the pages for
Miss Ramsey," Miles said stiffly. He took Phoebe's arm and
steered her to the piano when she rose from her chair.

"I hope you will excuse me from the game." Mr. Talbot's
manner was just as stiff as Miles' had been. "I find I am in no
mood for such frivolity. Perhaps, Miss Bywood will read aloud
one of Fordyce's sermons."

How dull was that? Even stranger was that my sister agreed
with him.

"My aunt and I will join you," Miss Darkin told me. Her aunt sent a puzzled frown towards her. "Though I hope you will not mind keeping the stakes low for us."

"Not at all, Miss Darkin," Ward said with unexpected gallantry. "Bywood will earn his money back from me another way. Perhaps you will do me the honor of being my partner."

"Good of you, Ward," I said as I took my seat at the card table. "I am confident, however, that Mrs. Darkin and I will manage to trounce you both."

My goal had been to discompose Mrs. Ramsey enough so that when Phoebe declared the engagement broken, there would be complete acceptance. Hopefully, I had done enough, though I suspected I was going to need a private conversation with Phoebe. The fool girl was making things difficult once again.

———— ◉ ————

DESPITE MY CONCERNS to the contrary, Rosamund had nothing to say from Lamridge to Bywood Hall. Philippa was in a thoughtful mood. The silence was a blessing after having to keep up a cheerful demeanor in front of the house party. George's well-sprung carriage kept my shoulder from being jostled too severely.

My sister-in-law stormed into the house and vanished from sight. Philippa followed at a slower pace, but once she was inside the hall, she spun to face me. "Luke, I need to speak to you," she said, sending a sharp glare at Miles. "Alone."

"Until morning, then," Miles told me quickly and then hurried off.

"Are you going to scold me here or will you allow me to go into the library for a glass of brandy?" I asked, glancing to where Butler was locking the front door. Apparently, George had returned already. "A man likes to fortify himself in the face of an unwarranted scolding."

My suggestion brought a scowl to my sister's face. "I think you've had plenty to drink, Lucas Bywood, if your behavior this evening is anything to go by."

Butler was watching us with obvious interest. Using my left hand, I took Philippa's elbow and steered her towards the library. "If you sincerely feel the need to rake me over the coals, sister dear, have the decency to avoid doing so in front of the servants. In front of guests is bad enough."

Wrenching free of my grip, Philippa spun to face me. "What is going on with you, Lucas?" she demanded. "Ever since you came home, you've been behaving strangely. You are quarrelsome, you are constantly drinking, and you have been quite rude. I am of a mind to tell Mama."

"I am not surprised," I said. "You always were one to carry tales to Mama and Father. Though, you may want to hurry if you want to be the first. I believe Rosamund has the same idea in mind."

My sister's lips thinned with anger. "Why will you not be serious for once?"

"You have never objected to my levity before." I raised an eyebrow at her. "Was this what Talbot was whispering in your ear all evening? What a disgrace of a brother I am to you? I had hoped he was doing the proper thing and whispering sweet endearments in your ear as a beau ought to do."

Eyes widening, Philly brought her hand up, and I caught her wrist before she could slap me. "This is cruel of you, Lucas!"

She couldn't know just how much pain I was in and cruelty had nothing to do with it. "You are being silly. You have my full permission to tell Mama about tonight. In fact, I urge you to do so. She will be very amused, and we both will laugh about it when I visit her tomorrow."

I released her wrist, and she backed up a few steps. Tears glistened in her eyes. "What happened to you, Lucas? You are not the brother I knew."

"Philippa, I want you to take a moment and think. If Father informed you that you were to marry someone you disliked, do you imagine that you would behave as though nothing was wrong?" Maybe that would give her something to think about.

Philippa shook her head. "You were behaving just fine a few days ago."

"There's only so long a man can be expected to act as though all is well when it is not."

I was tired and in pain. All I wanted was my bed and for this whole thing to be over. If I was being too sharp with my sister, I felt it was more than deserved. Philippa took a few more steps back, her eyes wide in her face. "You truly dislike Phoebe?" she asked, her tone tentative.

"Did I not make myself clear weeks ago? I find her to be a goosecap and a ninnyhammer. She is the last woman I would ever choose to marry."

She flinched, clasping her hands together. "Good night," she whispered before she rushed out of the room.

Sighing, I sent a look at the decanter that was temptingly within reach. I wanted to forget this entire evening, and more brandy would help that along. However, I knew that if I drank much more, I was not going to enjoy waking up in the morning. With reluctance, I left the brandy and the library.

Once I was in my room, I struggled to get undressed. No blood had seeped through the bandage, which was a relief. I stretched out on my bed and closed my eyes. The evening had been extremely taxing, but at least I had a hope of the charade finally coming to an end.

Chapter Sixteen

Later than usual the next morning, I dragged myself out of bed. Lukewarm water awaited me, and when I splashed it on my face, it helped drive the sleepiness away. It did nothing for the headache that pounded behind my eyes. I checked the stitches and found the skin reddened around them. I wound a bandage around it to protect it, hoping for the best.

Dressing was torture, and my hands shook by the time I was done. I spent several minutes seated on the edge of my bed, trying to steady myself and get my breath back. More than anything, I wanted to just cover myself with a blanket and let the world carry on without me.

However, the pretense that everything was as it should be needed to be kept up. Forcing myself to my feet, I made my way downstairs where I found the dining room empty. Once I filled a plate with food, I had little inclination of eating. Wearily, I sank into a chair and reached for the coffee.

I had barely managed a bite or two when the dining room door opened. Miles appeared, and his expression became stormy the moment he saw me. "It's about time you were up!" he declared, striding stowards me. "It would have served you right if I dragged you out of your bed."

"In case you've forgotten, I had the misfortune of being shot last night," I said, keeping my voice low. One never knew when a servant was nearby to overhear. Even speaking of the incident was a bad idea, but I had lost all patience with my friend. "I believe I am allowed to keep to my bed after such an occasion."

"How can you sleep knowing you have stolen the girl I intended to marry?"

My fork fell from my hand. "I beg your pardon?" As if I would steal Phoebe Ramsey from anyone.

"Phoebe is insisting that she will keep her word and marry you," Miles said, balling his hands into fists. Did he really wish to hit me after what had happened already? "She refused to see me this morning and sent Miss Darkin to tell me to leave her in peace."

I should have guessed. What was that girl thinking? Was she even capable of rational thought? "Phoebe said she had no wish to marry me, and I have not made her an offer of marriage."

"She has changed her mind."

Groaning, I leaned my head back and closed my eyes. "I will not marry her. I've said it from the start. While she might have changed her mind, I have not."

"I will not allow you to ruin her reputation!" Miles exclaimed.

Lifting my head, I opened my eyes to glare at him. "Miles, pay your debt to Lamotte, find a way to corner Phoebe somewhere, and propose to her. *You* said you had the matter in hand and that it was not on me to solve any of this."

Miles scowled and shook his head. "I'm of a mind not to repay Lamotte. After all, he lost the security, and I was forced to recover it myself. He should have accepted my payment earlier for he cannot force me to pay him now."

My thoughts went to Ward, who was waiting to be paid by Lamotte who in turn could not pay because he needed the payment from Miles. Could things get any more complicated? "Miles, I never imagined you would do anything so dishonorable. Go to Lamotte, tell him you have the ring, pay the man, and be done with the whole affair. Take it as a lesson for the future."

"And confess how I acquired the ring? Never! He would blackmail me for it; I am sure."

Peace and quiet were all I wanted. With desperate times calling for drastic measures, I made a swift decision. Perhaps I would regret it, but I'd had enough. "I will be engaging a cottage in Italy, and I will be moving there by the end of the year."

My friend's jaw dropped in shock. "Phoebe does not wish to live in Italy! You cannot force her to give up everything she knows just for your own selfish desires."

"Well, as I am not marrying Phoebe, I don't see how it concerns her."

My friend stated at me, his expression a mixture of fury and confusion. "Philippa is right. Travel has changed you."

With a frustrated growl, I pushed my chair back and stood up. Moving so quickly made everything spin, and I grabbed the table to steady myself. "I wish everyone would stop blaming my journey and saying it has changed me. I have not changed. Even if I hadn't gone abroad, I would not marry Phoebe Ramsey."

"Well, what else could be blamed for this selfish attitude? You weren't like this before. Since you returned, you have argued and been generally disdagreeable."

This time, it was my turn to stare at him. "My attitude confuses you? You know everything that has happened since I returned home. I learned of my mother's injury and poor health. I found myself expected to court and marry a silly, waspish chit of a girl for whom I have no fond regard. I have been shot. And despite all of this, everyone expects me to behave as though nothing is amiss."

"Do not speak of Miss Ramsey in such terms! She is an angel."

If I had not been in such pain, I would have thrown my hands in the air. "Even now, you do not even try to understand. Go and use your energy to convince your angel to marry you. I am done with our friendship, Miles. When you begin to use your brain once again, I will be happy to speak with you. Until then, I wish you all the best."

Miles' eyes widened and he opened his mouth to protest. However, I turned on my heel and walked out. I meant what I said. I was done with the whole thing.

———◈———

IT HAD BEEN YEARS SINCE I had been up to the nursery, but as Rosamund was insisting on improvements being made to many parts of the Hall, I felt the urge to go up before it was changed beyond recognition. It was, thankfully, the quietest area in Bywood Hall, now that there were no children in the house. I would have some peace there.

Sadly, I discovered that the furniture had already been removed. The toys I remembered from my childhood were gone as well. I had expected for there to be some sort of odor that would reveal how unused it was, but there wasn't. Mrs.

Jenson, the housekeeper, had been meticulous in keeping it clean.

I took a moment and just stood in the middle of the room, remembering my childhood. How much simpler everything had been then. How eager I had been to grow up and experience life.

When I made to leave, I spotted a small object half sitting on the window frame. Curious, I crouched down and picked it up.

"One of my wooden soldiers." I examined it, turning it over in my hand. It was one of twelve that I had often played with, right up until they disappeared when I was about seven years old. How often I had lined them up to fight some imaginary villain, especially when George had no interest in spending his time with me. "I wonder where the rest are."

"I hid them."

Startled, I glanced over my shoulder. My older brother was leaning against the doorframe of the room. He was watching me with a serious expression. Had he followed me up or simply guessed where he might find me?

"I was fond of these toys," I said to him. "Why did you hide them from me?"

"I once overheard our father remarking to Mother how fortunate it was that you enjoyed playing soldier since you would likely become one. I didn't like the idea of my only brother going off to fight a real war and potentially being killed. So, I hid them and encouraged you to find some other pastime."

Amazed, I shook my head. "I cried about these for weeks."

"Yes, I know. I was disappointed that you were such a baby about it. They're just toys, you know."

His tone was teasing, and we both chuckled. "Too bad nothing else ever took their place as my favorite," I said. There had been many games through the years that had entertained me, but I knew I would always look back on my toy soldiers as the most fun. My sisters' penchant for dolls had made them poor playmates for me, and George had enjoyed his lessons.

"You should have stuck to your books more: studied the law or to take the cloth. Made something of yourself."

Keeping the toy soldier in my hand, I straightened up. "Perhaps. But you have to admit school was pretty dull."

"Let's not argue, Luke."

I glanced at him. "If you are planning to berate me about my behavior as of late, I warn you that Philippa and Miles have already tried. Neither of them liked the outcome of these conversations."

George's jaw tensed, and he shook his head. "That they both tried to warn you about your behavior should tell you something."

"It tells me that neither of them understand me." I dropped my gaze to the soldier in my hand. "I suppose it shouldn't surprise me that you hid my toys. You always did want to control everything I did. Maybe I would have been better off becoming a soldier. Then, I would have had a logical reason to be away."

Immediately, George grabbed my arm. "Don't say things like that," he said. I glanced at the tight grip he had on me and felt thankful he was on my left and not my right. "If anything had happened to you—"

"Everyone would have mourned the loss of 'the spare,' but you would have provided your own heir in no time." I pulled away from him. "What is this about? Why did you follow me up here?"

"Philly told me what you said to her last night."

I couldn't hold back a laugh. "She said she was going to Mama, not you."

"I warned her long ago not to worry Mama about trivial matters," George said, waving his hand. "I want you to be honest with me. Do you honestly hate us all so much that you would live abroad?"

My reluctance to marry Phoebe was considered a 'trivial matter'? "I don't hate anyone, George. I do, however, dislike everyone trying to tell me how to live my life."

"Then, you don't hate Phoebe?"

A frustrated growl rose in my throat, and I wrenched my arm out of his grip. "Phoebe Ramsey is a silly girl, who cannot make up her mind about things. It would be beyond useless to hate her."

"Yet you're courting her, so there must be something you like about her," George pointed out with a note of triumph. Then, his eyes narrowed. "Or is this disagreeableness a ploy to force Phoebe to turn her attention elsewhere?"

There was that word again. Disagreeable was fast becoming a term I wished never to hear again. "Did Mama not speak to you about how you describe me? You only ever say I am 'disagreeable' when I choose to have my own opinion on a matter and that is wrong of you."

George's gaze shifted away. "I should have guessed it would be useless to try shielding you from harm," he said, his tone shifting to one of bitterness. "School made you independent, and your inheritance has only made your attitude worse. You only care for yourself."

Blowing out a breath, I turned to the window. Looking down, I saw Philippa walking in the garden. "I am a grown man, George, not a child with no notion of how to get on in the world. If I did not make my own decisions, what kind of man would I be? You and Father must realize this, and the sooner you do, the more peace we will all have in this family."

"Decisions have consequences. You might be grown, Luke, but you behave like a child. You do not stay in one place, and you do not consider how others are affected by what you do."

The conversation felt as though it were going around and around, with no end in sight. Neither of us was willing to bend. Not ten minutes earlier, we had been having such a pleasant moment of shared remembrance. "Did you come up here for a reason, or was it simply to argue about something we will never see eye to eye on?"

"It is not my fault that you choose to argue about everything."

My fault. Somehow, it was always my fault. Maybe the pain throbbing, not only in my head but my arm, was making me lose my patience quicker, but I was done. "Well, this has been fun, but I need to put Phaeton through his paces now. He is up against Ward's Tesoro tomorrow."

A race I was no longer looking forward to.

Scowling, George shook his head. "I don't like this friendship with John Ward. He has a poor reputation. I don't think you've heard the stories of what he's done in London, or how much he gambles."

"If everyone is to be believed, I have an equally bad reputation among our neighbors," I said with more sharpness than I'd intended. I slipped the toy soldier that had sparked this whole thing into my pocket. "As I do not deserve it, I reserve my opinion on Ward until I know his character. So far, my conversations with him have been pleasant and intelligent."

My words sent another flash of annoyance across George's face. I patted his shoulder. "I'll see you at dinner tonight."

"You're just going to run to our mother to complain some more, aren't you?"

Though I had planned on visiting Mama to apprise her of the situation, the implication that I only complained nettled my already frayed nerves. "I said I have to exercise Phaeton and that's exactly what I intend on doing."

As I strode out of the nursery, my muscles were tight. I tried to tell myself the situation wouldn't last much longer, but given how much had happened in the last week alone, the thought wasn't as reassuring as it should have been.

⟞⟝●⟞⟝

WHEN I ARRIVED AT THE stable, I knew I would not be able to ride Phaeton. The pain in my arm had grown with every jostling step I took. Instead, under the guise of desiring his opinion, I charged Geoff to take charge of my horse's exercise. Leaning against the fence, I watched with pride as they raced across the field.

If I lost the race, it would not be from any deficiency in Phaeton. The blame would rest solely with me. Well, technically, some blame should go to Miles for getting me hurt in the first place.

"He's in fine form, Mister Lucas," Geoff said when he rode Phaeton back. The groom dismounted and handed Phaeton's reins over to a stableboy. The boy led my horse off to cool down. "He'll give that Tesoro a run for his money."

Pleased that he agreed, I nodded. "He has never let me down in the past."

"Where will the race be taking place?"

I outlined the course Ward and I had agreed to: from the front of the Ramsey house to the road that stretched between Bywood Hall and Lamridge and then circling back across the open country. Geoff nodded, a thoughtful frown on his face. "Shall I ride the course early tomorrow to ensure no mischief has been done?"

The question startled me. My first instinct was to protest that neither Ward nor I would do anything dishonorable. Before I could voice those words, though, I recalled my mother's 'accident.' "If you would, Geoff," I said, keeping my voice low. "I shall give you my pistol to take with you. Just in case you need it."

"I appreciate it." Geoff shook his head. "I don't understand what's happened these past few months, Mister Lucas. First the mistress, then the break-in at Oakcrest, and now a highwayman? It just isn't right."

Surprised, I faced him. "Break-in? This is the first I've heard of this."

"It happened two weeks after the mistress and Sprite fell," Geoff said, sadness crossing his face at the memory. "Someone broke into Oakcrest and stole some valuables of Mr. Lamotte's. He dismissed the staff and brought new servants from London."

"That must have been a blow to many of the families in the neighborhood. Surely none of them were to blame."

"Nothing was ever proven. The constable questioned everyone and found no reason to blame them. Lamotte did not think that was good enough, so he dismissed them."

Thoughtfully, I allowed my gaze to shift in the direction of Oakcrest. Was it possible the robbery had been an invention of Lamotte? I returned my attention to the old groom. "What was taken?"

"Silverware, candlestick holders, and some food. A ring, too, I believe." Geoff glanced at the sky. "If there's nothing else, I'll be about my work."

With a nod, I dismissed him to his work. As I walked to the gardens, I thought about the new information. Had Lamotte invented the story to explain how he had lost Miles' ring? If that was the case, though, why had he not told Miles?

I thought everything had been sorted out, and now I couldn't be sure what this detail meant. I heaved a sigh. "Just typical."

Chapter Seventeen

B ecause Father didn't demand an explanation behind my proposed plan of moving to Italy, I guessed that he had not been told. A part of me dreaded the moment when he would learn of the scheme, due to his already strong dislike for my traveling. I did not doubt that the news, coupled with the fact that I was no longer courting Phoebe and thus would not be marrying her, would infuriate him.

As it was, I was pleased to be in his good favor for a rare moment. He could not have been more pleased with my actions to fix the Millers' roof. Besides his condemnation of the failure to locate the highwayman, it was all he wished to speak of at dinner. Apparently, when he rode around the estate, the Millers had praised me to the sky.

He didn't seem to hear Rosamund's snide comments on the subject. I was surprised and suspicious when my sister-in-law failed to enlighten him on my 'disagreeableness.' This was just the sort of thing I had expected her to use to her advantage, namely casting me in a bad light.

Philippa refused to meet my gaze all evening. Miles glowered at me with unconcealed anger matched only by George's irritation. Strange to have Father as the only person in charity with me.

There was nothing to keep me from going to my bed early that night and I did so, eager to escape the tense atmosphere of my family. In the privacy of my room, I discovered the skin around Skriven's stitches was red and irritated. Resolving to ask Mama discreetly about a possible poultice to keep infection at bay, I went to my bed for the night.

Nerves woke me just after dawn. My sleep had been fitful all night, and I barely felt rested. With my arm even sorer than the day before, I dressed and made my way downstairs. I disturbed one of the maids making up the fire in the hall, while a footman scurried through the green baize door. I passed the dining room and went out to the garden.

Dew glistened on the grass and dampened my boots as I walked. The smell of wet dirt and spring flowers filled the air. Early birds chirped in the trees with a few taking flight when I drew too close to their perches.

As I took it all in, I caught sight of Geoff riding towards the stables. The groom's worn face held a grimness I had never seen before. Abandoning my quest for peace, I changed my course and quickened my steps to meet him.

"You went out earlier than I expected," I said as I approached where Geoff had engaged a younger groom in conversation. At Geoff's nod, the other man hurried off. Curious, I asked, "Was the course clear?"

"It was not," Geoff said bluntly. In his hands was a length of rope. "I found two holes placed in front of the gates you and Mr. Ward will jump. And a line across the road in front of Oakcrest."

Worse than I had expected. Who had I managed to anger enough that they wanted to hurt, possibly kill, me?

"I'm sending Jim and Bobby to walk the course again. They'll fill in the holes and make sure no more mischief is done. I assume you cannot be persuaded to call off the race entirely."

Sighing, I shook my head. "You assume correctly. Thank you, Geoff."

"An opponent who cheats is not an honorable man."

I reached out and patted Geoff's shoulder. "I cannot prove it, but I am certain Mr. Ward would not stoop so low to win a friendly race. It may be the same man behind the hole that felled Mama is also the one behind this mischief."

Could it be Lamotte? He had already displayed antagonism towards Ward and me. I did not doubt he was willing to go to any length to keep us from interfering with what he saw as his affair.

"I will warn Ward, and we will both ride with care."

Geoff didn't look any less worried, but he gave a brief nod. He hurried on his way, and I returned to the garden. The hour I spent pacing there did nothing to calm my mind. I finally gave up the effort and went into breakfast.

Father and George were at the table when I walked in. "You're up early," Father said as I filled my plate. "It's gratifying to see your traveling didn't ruin the good routine your mother taught you."

"He is only up because he has a race today," George said before I could form a response.

I couldn't help but wince as I sat at Father's left hand. I had avoided telling him of the race for good reason. Father had only negative opinions on racing. When I dared to glance over, the disapproval was written on his face.

"Lucas, what does he mean?" he demanded.

"I'm sure it was mentioned before. One of the guests at Lamridge declared his mount superior to Phaeton," I said with as much calm as I was capable of displaying at the moment.

"We are meeting to settle the matter by means of a race. It is just a friendly competition."

"Your pride in your horse is unseemly."

"I cannot agree, Father. Phaeton comes from a good line and is a sweet-goer. Why should I not be proud of him?"

With a scoff, Father rose from his seat, food still on his plate. "As ever, my opinion holds no weight with you," he said as though I had not spoken. "If you come to harm from this ill-advised venture, it is on your head, and you will get no sympathy from me."

As he strode out, I said under my breath, "I would expect nothing less."

"What did you say?"

Swiftly, I glanced at my brother. His expression was entirely too smug. "I suppose I ought not to expect you to be there to cheer me on," I said, turning my attention back to my breakfast. "I understand you want to stay in Father's good opinion."

"When Father is so against it? I won't be anywhere near that race."

"Your filial support is unmatched."

A loud thud made everything rattle on the table as George's fist slammed into the thick oak of the table. "Why must you treat everything as though it were a jest of some kind?" he asked, his voice taut with anger.

"I will not argue with you, George," I said with a sigh. "I suggest that we both keep our own counsel until we are finished eating. I, for one, am not inclined to forego a meal to revisit a topic we will never see eye-to-eye on."

He threw down his fork and stood up. "You are impossible," he said, looking down on me. George walked out of the room and slammed the door behind himself.

"Well, if this is what it takes to get some peace and quiet, it is almost worth it," I said half-heartedly to the empty room.

AN HOUR BEFORE THE appointed time for the race, I walked Phaeton to Lamridge . When I arrived there, I found Ward at the stable, checking Tesoro's tack. He came over to shake my hand, looking more animated than I had ever seen him.

Concisely, I informed him of the problems Geoff had encountered and of the measures my family's grooms were taking to keep the course clear. Ward scowled and shook his head. "The lengths some people will go to avoid repaying a debt," he said disdainfully. "It is nothing less than criminal."

"You believe it is Lamotte's doing?"

"I can think of no other person who could have anything to gain."

It was no comfort to hear my own suspicions stated by another person. As if sensing my concern and unease, Ward shifted the conversation to the races and the bloodlines of this year's winners. He knew much more on the matter than I did due to being present in person for the races.

As the start time drew close, Mr. Ramsey and Miss Darkin came from the house to spectate. The older gentleman informed me in a low voice he desired an audience with me immediately after the race was concluded. From his grave expression, I gathered he had been told my plans for the future and wished to talk me out of them.

At least one thing was going to plan.

Cheerfully, Miss Darkin wished us both luck and cautioned us, in polite, tactful terms, not to be idiots.

While Ward mounted Tesoro, my family's carriage arrived. Philippa came into view first and, to my shock, was followed by a sullen George and Rosamund. "We have come to wish you luck, Luke," my younger sister said as she rushed to my side. She patted Phaeton's neck. "Mama desires a detailed account of your win."

If Mama had ordered George and Rosamund to come, it was no wonder they appeared angry. Miles joined them, his expression neutral. I nodded at them before smiling at Philippa. "Thank you, Philly. Though my victory is not assured, you know. Tesoro is a fine steed and Ward a worthy opponent."

I pulled myself into the saddle, feeling a twinge of pain from my injury as I did so, and then nudged Phaeton into motion. Ward and I lined up in the middle of the driveway. Mr. Ramsey held his pocket watch in his right hand, his left upraised. As if they sensed the excitement and tension, Tesoro and Phaeton kept shifting, eager to be off.

"Bywood, if there should be a trap or some kind of sabotage, we call the race off," Ward said abruptly in a low voice I barely heard. "There is no need for either of us to risk injury."

Startled, I sent a glance in his direction. At that moment, out of the corner of my eye, I saw Mr. Ramsey bring his hand down. Tesoro surged forward as I swung my focus back. Phaeton responded to my kick, and we were off!

A delighted laugh filled my throat as we drew closer to Ward and Tesoro. My opponent must have heard me for he glanced over his shoulder. For a moment, the expression on his face was one of open amusement. An answering laugh floated back to my ears as he refocused on the race.

Once we were on the road, where it was straight and relatively smooth, I was able to make up for my poor start. Phaeton needed no urging to increase his speed and drew abreast with Tesoro. Ward didn't even glance my way this time, and my competitive spirit flared into action.

Several spectators were along the road, waving and cheering as we went past. Though I didn't give them much attention, I had the suspicion that most of them were from my family's estate and were cheering for me. I did, as I passed the edge of the Miller cottage, raise my hand at them and excited shouts sounded behind me.

Phaeton edged past Tesoro, and I could hear Ward speaking to his horse. I took the lead, determined to keep it. However, I recognized the border of Oakcrest, and I reined Phaeton back. To his credit, Ward didn't try to take advantage. "Lamotte?" I heard him ask.

Glancing over, I gave a brief nod. When I refocused on the stretch of road in front of us, I let out a shout. Three children had run out into the road not more than ten yards in front of us. Ward's exclamation included language Mama would never have approved of.

The smallest child, a girl no more than three years old, screamed, her eyes as round as saucers. Phaeton reacted to the shrill sound, trying to lock his legs. I jerked on the reins, knowing that to come to a stop was not an option. My poor horse objected to the whole thing and reared onto his back legs.

It was in vain that I tried to remain in the saddle. My wounded arm gave out and, as my luck would have it, I landed on it when I hit the ground. A pained cry left my lips as Phaeton trotted off the road.

Blackness filled my vision as I tried to force the pain down. After a few moments, I became aware of someone speaking over me. Blinking, I focused on Ward's face where worry and concern were written.

"Have you broken something?" he asked, seeming to realize I understood what he was saying.

"I don't think so," I said honestly. The only pain was coming from the bullet wound, and I suspected I had torn the stitches. In fact, I could feel warm blood trickling down my arm. "None of the children were hurt, were they?"

"No, and they've run off back the way they came," he said with a scowl. He offered his hand to help me up. "They ought to know better than to run into the road like that. A horseman with lesser skill would not have been able to avoid striking them."

Accepting his help, I got back on my feet. "Somehow, I don't think it was completely their idea."

Ward's eyes darkened with anger. "Lamotte has gone too far if he is inciting children to endanger themselves," he said, balling his hands into fists. "And for what? A miser like him would have only offered them a penny or two, I am sure."

"Let's not jump to conclusions." Turning, I spotted Phaeton nibbling at grass alongside the road. "If it's all the same to you, Ward, perhaps we can postpone this race until we can be sure no one will attempt to sabotage it?"

"You took the words right out of my mouth." Ward sent one last glare at the property before facing me. "You are uninjured?"

Ruefully, I nodded, though my arm was sending streaks of pain down to my fingertips. "Nothing worse than bruised pride," I said, anxious to turn his attention away from me.

The intense fury fading from his eyes, Ward gave a scoff. "Somehow, I don't think that is true, Bywood. Come along. We may as well return ourselves to Lamridge and tell the others what happened."

***

WHEN WE TROTTED UP to Lamridge , I groaned as I saw the small crowd that had gathered. Confused looks and questions were exchanged as we drew closer. "What's this then?" Mr. Ramsey asked, hurrying to meet us.

"Regrettably, there was an unfortunate incident involving Bywood and a trio of unthinking children," Ward said, swinging down. I followed suit a moment later. "Therefore, we agreed to put off the race until another time."

"How provoking!" Rosamund said with a pout. "We were all dragged out here for nothing? I do hope you scolded the children soundly and punished them."

"Mrs. Bywood, you are so unfeeling!" Miss Darkin said, her tone horrified. "Mr. Bywood, please tell me the children came to no harm."

"Ward assured me that all three ran off on their own," I said to her. I raised my voice as I glanced around the crowd. "I apologize that you all came out expecting a definitive end to our race. Ward and I will complete our friendly competition another day."

To my surprise, the worry did not leave Miss Darkin's face. "Why, Mr. Bywood! You are bleeding!"

Every gaze focused on me and I lifted my hand, realizing at that moment that my fingers were sticky. Sure enough, blood had run down my arm, coming into view on the back of my hand. Many inappropriate words ran through my mind as I raised my head. "Thank you for your concern, Miss Darkin," I said, striving and failing for a light tone. "It's nothing."

"Luke! Why did you not say something?" Philippa let go of Mr. Talbot's arm and rushed to me. Rather roughly, she grabbed onto my arm and examined the sleeve of my jacket, clinging tightly as I tried to get away from her. "Mr. Ward, how could you allow him to ride back like this?"

"He said he was unharmed," Ward said to defend himself. He held his hands up and took a step back as if to distance himself from the situation. "If he chose to keep such information to himself, it is obviously not serious. He rode the whole way back here with no trouble."

"I am fine," I said, grateful to have him on my side. "Philly, let it go. It's nothing you need to worry about."

"Why, there is not a rip or tear! How is this possible?" Philippa asked, her voice puzzled. She stared at me, a frown creasing her forehead. "How can you be bleeding but not have any damage to your sleeve?"

Rosamund gave a loud gasp and brought her hand to her chest. "He was injured before the race!" she announced dramaticaly. She spun and grabbed George's arm. "Mr. Bywood, did you not say you shot one of the highwaymen?"

George gave a start. "Surely you don't think—"

However, my sister-in-law was not to be deterred or reasoned with. "Lucas Bywood is the highwayman!"

Chapter Eighteen

Dead silence spread across the yard at Rosamond's exclamation. I cleared my throat, trying to think of some way to escape the sudden scrutiny. "That's a ridiculous accusation, Rosamund. Why would I need to hold you up and steal a ring from you?"

Rosamund's chin came up with defiance. "You have never liked me," she said, a sob coming into her voice. She covered her face with her hands. "You want only to torment me!"

"A fine reason to risk getting shot," I said, lacing my voice with all the scorn I could muster. As I glanced over the crowd, I realized that Miles wasn't where he'd been standing not five minutes earlier. Had he left me to deal with this on my own? "If you ask me, Rosamund, you have been reading too many novels."

Ward gave a loud, exaggerated laugh and said, "Had I known my little story last week would send the ladies' imagination running wild, I would have kept it to myself. I will have to remember this for the future. Now, Mrs. Ramsey, have you some refreshment? Bywood and I are famished from our ride, and I'm sure everyone else is parched from waiting for our return."

At least I had someone on my side. Mrs. Ramsey, though, made no move to offer refreshments. No one seemed to pay Ward any heed. "There's an easy way to prove Rosamund wrong," George said. "Remove your jacket, Lucas. Show us the injury."

Dread ran through me. Ward met my eyes, and he shook his head. Feeling as though I had been backed into a corner, I said, "I will not." It would prove nothing, only that I had been shot. "I am not a highwayman or a thief."

My quiet statement seemed only to confirm my guilt in their minds. Rosamund let out a scream and proclaimed she always knew I was good for nothing. Mrs. Ramsey began fluttering her hand in front of her face and gasped for breath as Mrs. Darkin tried to calm her. Mr. Talbot pulled Philippa away as though proximity to me would infect his wife-to-be with dangerous tendencies. Phoebe stared at me as though she was confused and George shook his head mournfully.

"I didn't take the ring," I said, raising my voice to be heard over the din. "I have no need for it or any desire to have it."

"If you are not the highwayman, as you claim, then why do you not show your arm?" Rosamund asked. She stepped forward to jab her finger into my chest. "I want my ring back, you thief!"

Irritated, I swatted her hand away as I would an annoying insect. "Did you not hear me? I didn't take it. Why would I? What reason would I have to steal something you would recognize the moment you saw it?"

"Lucas, you will come home with me now," George said in a low voice. "I'm sure our father will want to hear a full account of your recent mischief."

Miss Darkin stepped forward. "Someone must go for the doctor," she insisted. "Mr. Bywood is still bleeding, after all."

George grabbed onto my uninjured arm as though he expected me to run away or otherwise try to escape. "Thank you, Miss Darkin," he said, making her bristle with his dismissive tone. "I know how to take care of my brother. Mr. Ramsey, if it is not too much trouble, please have Phaeton delivered to our stable and send someone for Dr. Morgan."

The older man gave a nod, his expression one of disappointment.

"You cannot mean to take the criminal in the carriage with us!" Rosamund said, aghast. "I do not want him anywhere near me!"

"I can see no other alternative, my dear," George told her. "I will ensure he does nothing to you."

What did he imagine I would do in a carriage? Assault her? Insult her? "I can ride Phaeton back myself," I said. "I have no intention of fleeing the country. I have done nothing wrong."

George's fingers tightened. "Why should I believe you? You have clearly been lying to us all."

"It would be my pleasure to escort Mrs. Bywood and Miss Bywood home once they have had a chance to recover from this shock," Mr. Talbot offered. "Mrs. Ramsey, no doubt, could use their company for a few hours."

"Thank you, sir." With more force than was necessary, George pushed me towards the carriage. He remained far too close for comfort as I climbed in. He was quick to get in and close the door.

"Will you listen to reason now?" I asked as the carriage began moving. "I swear I did not take the stupid ring. Yes, I was in the trees, and yes, you shot me. I had nothing to do with Rosamund's ring being taken from her, though."

His silence gave me my answer. Closing my eyes, I leaned my head against the cushion. How had everything gone so wrong, so quickly?

Miles had better be on hand when I arrived at the Hall to set things right.

———◆———

GEORGE KEPT A GRIP on the back of my jacket, ignoring my protest over such treatment, and marched me into the Hall. "Butler, is my father in his office?" he asked.

"He is not," Butler said, his face barely registering surprise. "He went to inspect the Millers' new roof. Is there a problem, Mr. Bywood?"

My brother groaned. "Dr. Morgan should be arriving soon. Tell him that my unfortunate brother was shot a few days ago and send him to my father's office."

I managed a grin when Butler's eyes widened with astonishment as he glanced towards me. "George is making too much of a small thing," I said. I did not doubt that Dr. Morgan would put two and two together and figure out what had happened. "In fact, you could just send Mr. Russell's valet, Skriven, down and he will patch me back up in no time."

"I'm afraid Mr. Russell left with his valet no more than fifteen minutes ago," Butler said stoically. "He did not say if he intended to return, but he did take all of his luggage with him."

Before I could question the butler anymore, George pushed me towards Father's office. I didn't put up a fight as I analyzed the news. Miles had just left? There was no possible way he could have missed that his idiotic highwayman scheme had landed me in further trouble. Under the circumstances, I felt I had every right to explain his part in the whole thing.

"Sit down and stay there," George said, shoving me into the closest chair. "We are going to stay here until Father returns."

"And while we wait, I can explain to you—"

"You will say nothing! I am in no mood for any tall tale of yours."

Pressing my lips together, I settled myself more comfortably in the chair. George paced in front of me, sending anxious glances at the door. Much to my relief, we didn't have long to wait. "What is this about?" Father asked as he entered. "Lucas! Are you bleeding? What happened?"

"The doctor will be here soon," George said before I could respond. "Lucas has been keeping secrets from us. Again. He was one of the two men I saw among the trees the night Rosamund and I were held up. He was the highwayman."

Father's eyes flicked from George to me and seemed to make the connection. "Are you telling me you shot your brother?"

Flustered, George sputtered for a moment. "No! Well, yes, but that's not the point." He waved a hand at me. "Lucas was one of the highwaymen who took Rosamund's ring. He has been foolish, irresponsible, and everything we feared his inheritance would make him."

It took all my self-control to keep from taking offense at the last statement. I needed to remain focused on the topic at hand and resolve this misunderstanding. "I have told you I'm not a highwayman," I said, straightening myself in the chair. "It was Miles' scheme. I had no part in it."

"You cannot blame your friend when he isn't here to defend himself." Father frowned at me as he spoke. He moved closer and reached as though he would take my arm. His hand dropped before he touched me. "Lucas, George, what is this all about? I thought you were risking your life in a senseless race."

"Oh, I was," I said before George could cause any more damage with his 'explations.' "Until children from Oakcrest—I think they were Charles Simmons' children, but I did not have a good look—ran into our path and I fell from Phaeton. Ward and I agreed to postpone our race until another time. We returned to Lamridge , and suddenly I'm the highwayman."

"If you're so innocent, why didn't you agree to remove your coat at Lamridge ?" George asked, his tone frustrated. "You're not treating this matter with any degree of seriousness. Have you any idea what the consequences are for committing highway robbery?"

"I didn't steal anything! How many times must I repeat myself?"

Heaving a sigh, Father said at the same time, "I hardly think this has to go beyond the ones who already are aware of it, George. Lucas will return the ring, and we will say no more about it."

Why was I not surprised Father did not believe me? "I don't have the ring because I didn't take it."

George crossed his arms. "You can't have sold it already, Luke. You've not gone anywhere, so do not think you can pull the wool over our eyes."

"Search my room. You won't find it."

"Well, then, you've hidden it somewhere else."

My anger growing, I pushed myself up, hissing as pain warned me I was using my arm too much. "Why will you not believe me? Miles is the one who took the ring."

"And why would he do that?" Father asked. "Sit down, Lucas, before you fall over."

I was not on the verge of collapsing, but I sat down anyway. "I don't know why Miles would do something so idiotic," I said, even though I did know. Miles had thought it the only option to get his ring back and to be able to offer for Phoebe finally. "It's quite a tangle. The ring is an heirloom of the Russel family. I don't know how Rosamund ended up with it since Miles used the ring as security for a debt he owes to Mr. Lamotte."

"Are we supposed to believe that?" George scoffed.

The office door opened, interrupting our 'discussion.' "Dr. Morgan has arrived, sir," Butler said.

"Send him in," Father said. "George, while the doctor is tending to your brother's injury, search Lucas' room. If you find the ring, bring it to me."

Part of me wanted to protest the intrusion into my personal space, but I had challenged them to do it. And, it was slightly encouraging that Father had used the word 'if' and not 'when.' Perhaps he wasn't entirely convinced of my guilt.

Scowling, George said, "I will take a few of the footmen to help with—"

"I think the fewer who know about this, the better."

I couldn't keep the smirk from my lips as my brother stormed out. "And you ought not to look so amused, young man," Father said sharply. He rose from his seat and moved around his desk. "I don't understand what you have gotten yourself into, but I do know you are in the middle of something."

Dr. Morgan entered, carrying his medical bag. "I'm told young Lucas has had something of a mishap."

"You could call it that," Father said, extending his hand. "The fool boy got himself shot two days ago and said nothing."

"I can answer for myself," I said, objecting to being talked over. "I'm sitting right here."

"It's a wonder you're even doing that if the bloodstain is anything to go by," the doctor said as he set his bag down by my chair. "A fool is the only one who would even try to hide a bullet wound."

The following hour was even worse than when Skriven had stitched the wound shut. Dr. Morgan ruthlessly scrubbed my arm before he threaded a needle. Father relented enough to hand me a full measure of brandy, which eased some of the pain.

George slunk in halfway through Dr. Morgan's needlework and admitted that he had found nothing in my room. His disappointment was obvious, and I couldn't decide if I should be relieved he had found nothing or offended he had been so sure of my guilt. He poured himself a drink and held his silence.

Dr. Morgan wrapped my arm, and then left, leaving behind a sleeping draft for 'the shock.' I was faced once again with my father and brother. "So, now what?" I asked. It wasn't merely the alcohol that made me flippant. "Do we begin again? I say I am innocent and you proclaim me to be a liar?"

"Lucas, enough," Father said with a sigh. He drew his hand over his eyes, and I noticed for the first time that he was looking older. The lines around his eyes and the creases in his forehead were from stress. "No one is accusing you."

"He could have hidden the ring," George said, his tone defensive. "How else do you explain him getting shot?"

"He has already said he was in the trees," Father said, much to my surprise. "No doubt he heard you shooting and thought he ought to look into it. Hardly an intelligent idea, but absolutely the foolish sort of course I can see Lucas taking."

Again, I didn't know whether to be flattered he knew me so well or offended at being described as foolish. It took too much energy to feel anything at all. Father faced George with a determined expression. "One way or another, we will get to the bottom of this."

"Don't tell me, after all Lucas has done, you trust anything he says," George said with disbelief.

My irritation dissipated as my gaze met Father's. "However irresponsible he may have acted in the past, he has never been a liar," he said. "George, send a message to Mr. Lamotte and request a moment of his time."

Finally, it was not all on my shoulders. I blew out a sigh of relief. "And what about Lucas?" George asked, his tone almost amusing with how petulant he sounded.

"Lucas is going to his room, and he will stay there until I have learned the truth."

With the effects of falling from Phaeton —and getting my arm resewn—clouding my mind, I couldn't find any annoyance at being sent to my room like a child. My room meant my bed, where I could sleep.

With any luck, when I woke up, this whole situation would be resolved.

A FIVE-HOUR NAP DID wonders for restoring my mood. Given how long it had been since I had last eaten, my stomach rumbled as I sat up. With a yawn, I pushed myself out of bed and made myself respectable before I walked to the door. Strangely, I found a letter on the floor and knelt down to pick it up.

With one hand, I broke the seal, and with the other, I made to open the door. It didn't budge.

"Odd," I said aloud, jiggling the knob. I blamed fatigue for how long it took me to realize the door was actually locked. "I don't believe this."

I hit the door with my fist. "Hey! Is there anyone there?"

No one answered me. I had been locked away like a criminal.

Chapter Nineteen

I pounded on the door for nearly ten minutes before I gave it up as useless. Groaning, I collapsed onto my bed. The letter in my other hand crinkled, reminding me of its presence. As it seemed I wasn't going anywhere, I unfolded it. The handwriting was as familiar to me as my own, and I chuckled as I read.

'My dear little brother,

I find myself quite astonished at the remarkable news your last letter imparted to me. An arranged marriage? With Phoebe Ramsey, no less! What is our father thinking? I mean no disrespect, but clearly, he has not considered this as he ought. Miss Ramsey is, I am sure, a lovely young lady, however, she always was a silly thing. Hardly the type of girl for you.

I have no doubt Mama is as appalled by this as I am, and she in a situation where she cannot assist you! Never fear, dear brother, I will come to your rescue. You say that Miss Ramsey is capable of breaking the agreement with no repercussion? Well, I shall simply devise a way of convincing her to do just that.

Inform our parents that I am coming. Julia and Tristan are ecstatic to visit their grandparents, and I am confident they will raise Mama's spirits...'

Chuckling, I folded my older sister's letter. "Oh, Jane," I said aloud. How surprised she would be when she arrived to discover I had managed to get myself into a worse tangle than an arranged marriage.

There was a light tap on the door. "Luke? Are you awake?"

"Philippa?" I asked, recognizing the voice of my sister. Hastily, I rose and hurried to the door. "Yes, I am awake."

The doorknob jiggled. "Why is your door locked? Luke, let me in so we can talk."

"Unfortunately, I cannot do that. I didn't lock myself in. Find Butler or Mrs. jenson. They're sure to have a key to open the door."

I heard Philippa's gasp through the wood. "Never say you have been locked in! This is horrible!"

Sighing, I leaned my head against the door. "Did you need something? Has Mr. Ramsey returned Phaeton with no trouble?"

"How can you be concerned about your horse when you have been accused of a crime?" Philippa asked, her tone one of astonishment.

"I am innocent of any wrongdoing." There was a long moment of silence. "You don't believe me, do you."

"Of course I do," she said, much too quickly for me to believe her sincerity. "You should have been there, Lucas! Mr. Ward scolded Rosamund for causing a hum. Mrs. Ramsey says that she has never seen him come to anyone's defense before. Everyone is so confused about the whole situation.

"How did this happen, Luke?" Philippa abruptly asked, her tone serious all of a sudden.

I lifted my head from the door. "In short, Miles and Phoebe have an attachment, however, Miles lost a family heirloom in a wager with Mr. Lamotte," I said, eager to tell anyone the tale. "Miles concocted a wild scheme to take back his ring from Rosamund by pretending to be a highwayman—though how she came to have the ring is beyond me. I happened upon him at the wrong time and was shot for simply being in the area."

There was silence from the other side. If only I could see her face to know what she was thinking! "Would you be able to relate this whole situation to Mama before George or Rosamund have a chance to blacken my reputation completely?" I asked.

"Luke, I don't think Mama needs to know about this. She will fret about it, and her health will suffer."

"Keeping Mama in the dark will not help her health either," I said, far more sharply than I should have. "How would you feel if you were confined to one room for months on end with nothing to occupy your mind?"

Again, there was a long silence. I could only hope that she was thinking about what I had said. Of all my sisters, Philippa was never one to have any depth of thought on most subjects. "Oh, and you should make preparations for Jane's arrival," I said, reminded of my older sister's letter. "She is bringing Julia and Tristan, though she failed to mention whether her husband will accompany her as well."

I heard Philippa exclaim, "Oh, it's just like Jane to not send word ahead! And I suppose she gave no indication exactly when she would arrive? She will land on us tomorrow for all I know! Of all the thoughtless things to do!"

My younger sister's tirade made me smile. "Philippa!" I finally said, trying to get her attention. "When you tell Mama about what has happened to me, add in how Jane is coming. She will send for Mrs. Jensen, and all will be arranged. Do not leave it for Rosamund to handle."

"I would never make such a mistake as that," Philippa said, sounding offended I would even suggest she would leave it to our sister-in-law. "I ought to go, Luke. It will be dinner soon. I'll come back tomorrow morning if you haven't been released then. If there's anything you need, you must tell me."

"Have a good evening," I said as I heard her footsteps in the hallway. Shaking my head, I walked to the window to look out. The sun had started to dip towards the horizon, and shadows were growing long on the ground. I had slept the afternoon away. "I hope someone thinks to let me out for food, or send me up a tray."

———— ◉ ————

NEARLY TWO HOURS LATER, there was a knock on my door and then the click of the lock turning. I lifted my gaze from the book I had been reading. Mrs. Jensen stepped in and, without making eye contact, carried a tray to my table. Without saying a word, she hurried back to the door and pulled it closed behind her.

The lock clicked once again, and once again I was trapped in my room. I had, for a brief moment, considered an escape through my window, but had put it to the back of my mind as a worst-case option. In truth, I knew it would have been a foolish and ill-advised plot.

In the light of a single candelabra, I ate every morsel from my tray. Once again left with nothing to do, I picked up the book. I had no notion as to how it had ended up in my room as it wasn't the usual type of book I would read. It was the first volume of a rather amusing novel entitled *Pride and Prejudice*.

Not long after I had taken up the book, I heard the lock on my door click. Expecting it to be Mrs. Jensen or one of the maids come to retrieve the tray, I kept my eyes on the printed words. Thus, I gave a start when I heard my sister-in-law's voice.

"Aren't you so quick to be lazy?"

Lifting my head, I sent a glare towards her. "I don't recall inviting you into my room, Rosamund."

"A criminal loses his right to anything," she said, her tone prim. She put her hands on her hips. "It was suggested that you might be amenable to returning my ring if I requested it in person. Return it to me now."

A laugh left my lips. "Oh, Sister Rosamund. Is this how you make requests? It sounds more like a demand. Even if I had taken it, I wouldn't hand it over to you just like that."

Her eyes narrowed, and a scowl marred her face. "I knew you were a disagreeable, irresponsible young man, but this is outside of enough! Were I not aware of how it would reflect on my dear Mr. Bywood's good name, I would gladly watch you hang."

"I am curious as to how you acquired the ring in the first place," I commented, ignoring her threat. "I know George did not give it to you. In fact, it was used as security for a gambling debt."

Her eyes widened with anger. "My brother is no gambler!" she said, her voice raising an octave.

"Did I mention your brother's name? I don't believe I did. However, it is telling that his is the first name you bring up."

With a gasp, Rosamund took a step back, her face going pale. "How dare you?"

"How dare I?" I rose from my seat. "I am not the one making wild accusations and demands. I do not know what induced my brother to marry you, but you would do well to cease your efforts to cause a division between my family and me."

Her right hand came up as though she wished to slap me. "You-you!" she stammered.

"The truth of the matter will come out, Rosamund," I said, lowering my tone. "I suggest you keep your opinions to yourself until that time. Kindly leave my room now."

"You are as abominable as you were in London!"

"I don't know about that. You are not the first to mention a meeting in London. If it happened, I do not recall it happening. I'm sure I would have remembered someon as sharp tongued as you. Now would you kindly leave and allow me to return to my book?"

Face red with fury, she spun on her heel and stalked to the door. The door rattled with how hard she pulled it closed behind her. With a sigh, I sank back down and leaned my head back against my pillow.

Apparently, Miles had not reappeared to clear my name, which I found to be the most dishonorable thing he had ever done. Right up there with pretending to be a highwayman robbing my brother and sister-in-law. Whether Father and George had interrogated Lamotte for the truth of the matter, I had no way of knowing.

And how long my imprisonment in my room would last, I couldn't even begin to guess.

THOUGH THE NOVEL WAS entertaining, I ended up falling asleep earlier than usual. Thus, I rose just after dawn. As long as I had been in my bed, I had gotten little rest with my arm aching as badly as it had. Dr. Morgan's sleeping draft still stood on the table beside my bed, but I had little inclination to take the opiate. Who knew if would need my wits to defend myself?

My stomach rumbled as I stared out the window. I seemed to have been forgotten for no one came with a tray to break my fast. It was nearing ten o'clock when I heard a loud commotion in the hallway. I faced the door in anticipation of being freed.

The door was unlocked and swung open. "Luke!" My oldest sister, Jane, held her hands out as she hurried in. "What an abominable mess this all is! How have you borne it?"

As I took her hands, an unearthly rumble sounded from my stomach. Jane's eyes widened. "Have they been starving you as well?" she demanded in outrage. "I cannot believe the state of things in this house! It is beyond comprehension!"

With a laugh, I shook my head. "It is not as bad as you are making it out to be, Jane," I said. She frowned at me and opened her mouth to speak. I squeezed her hands to cut her off. "There has been a misunderstanding, that is all. I have every confidence it will be put right soon enough. Let me explain what has happened."

"I have had the full story from Mama, and another version from Philippa, and an entirely different account from George and Rosamund," Jane said, pulling her hands free. "I think I have pieced together the truth. Your friend Miles has landed you in a fix once again and has left you to take the blame for it. How many times did I tell you he was no good?"

"His actions may have been rash and irresponsible, but he is far from being 'no-good,' Jane. He had his reasons for his actions. I only regret he sacrificed our friendship along the way."

My sister sighed and shook her head. "And still you defend him. Very well, Luke. I will speak no more against your friend, though my opinion of him has not changed. Now come. Let's get you fed and then we will see about resolving this matter before the whole county knows of it."

"I would be greatly surprised if the whole county doesn't already know of it," I said, following her to the door. In the hallway, there was no sign of the footmen who must have accompanied Jane to my room. "How did you arrive so early? I was not expecting you until this afternoon at the earliest."

"When I went to Charles about this, he agreed there was no time to lose," she said, referring to her husband of eight years. I followed her along the corridor. "I do delight in setting Butler and Mrs. Jensen on their ears with a sudden arrival, you know. And what is this I hear about the nursery being unavailable?"

"Rosamund wished to renovate it in anticipation of her own children."

Jane scowled and shook her head. "I cannot understand what induced George to marry that woman. She is everything that is disagreeable."

Again, I laughed. It was a relief to have my sister by my side and to be free of my room. "You cannot know just how many times that word has been used to describe me. I am just shy of being a confirmed reprobate."

"Yes, I've heard some of what Rosamund has been saying about you, and believe me she and I will be having words about it as soon as Mama is finished with her," Jane said, her tone dark with anger. She heaved a sigh. "If this is what happens when I am away, I shall simply have to convince Talbot to purchase a house in the neighborhood so I can manage things."

"It is simply a matter of bad timing. Had Mama been in good health, I am certain none of this would have happened."

"Well, the children and I will be here for at least a month. We shall see what we can do about getting Mama back on her feet and returning the house to normalcy. In the meantime, shall we clear your name before or after breakfast?"

"After. You know I detest missing a meal."

———— ◉ ————

CHARLES CASTLETON JOINED us at the table, though it was only to drink some coffee. He was the most amiable of my brothers-in-law. He had a quickness of mind and good humor that made him easy to get along with. His fortune was modest and he had no land. He and Jane had spent most of their married life in London as he sought a suitable estate.

He and Jane made no mention of the situation, keeping the conversation to the estates they had toured and the failings they contained. It was in the middle of a description of a poor stable that Father appeared. "There you are, Luke," he said, his gaze landing on me. "I'd wondered where I would find you. You've been keeping to yourself too much."

I raised my eyebrow at that. "Not by choice, I assure you."

"And what is that supposed to mean?"

"Papa, you will not believe how I discovered Luke this morning," Jane said, jumping to her feet. "He had been locked in his room, and no one had deemed it right to take him breakfast. Such treatment is unjust! How could you have allowed it to happen?"

Father's eyes narrowed. "Locked in his room?"

"I awoke yesterday afternoon to find myself locked in," I said, realizing he'd had no part in my imprisonment. "I assumed it was a precaution on your part to keep me from fleeing the country. George seemed to think it likely that I would do so."

"This has gone on long enough," Father said, his tone a growl. He strode to the door. "Butler! See to it that all members of the family are assembled in the drawing room in half an hour."

Chapter Twenty

It was quite a group of us that gathered in the drawing room right before the appointed time. Mama was even there, sitting in front of the fire with a shawl around her shoulders. She had only glares for Rosamund and George who sat on the edge of the room. Jane and Castleton sat side by side on the sofa, incongruously in the middle of everything though they had the least to do with it than anyone.

"Where is Papa?" Philippa asked with an obvious pout. "I am promised to walk with Mr. Talbot in an hour."

"I'm sure your Mr. Talbot will wait," Jane said, her tone sharp with irritation. "There are more important things at hand, Philly."

"No, she is right," George said, sending a glare at Jane who was two years older than him. "We have all of us better things to do than sit around."

"Children, kindly remember your manners," Mama said patiently. "You are all of an age where I shouldn't have to remind you."

"If this meeting results in my receiving my ring back, I will gladly submit to anything," Rosamund said, pointedly glaring at me. "Justice must be done!"

I chose not to respond to her statement as I had defended myself enough already, and had little energy to do so yet again. Not when she clearly had no inclination to listen. George only had ears for her, and everyone else in the room was, to varying degrees, on my side.

"So which of you two is to blame for locking me in my bedchamber?" I asked instead, glancing between George and Rosamund. "Father has already denied knowing anything about it. Philly also had no hand in confining me. So you are the only two left who have not been acquitted."

Mama's eyes narrowed. "George?"

My brother fidgeted as everyone focused on him and Rosamund. "I—may have overstepped," he said. "I have nothing more to say on the matter other than I did what I thought was right at the time."

"Ah, good. You're all here," Father said as he came through the doorway, preventing any of us from pursuing the matter. He stepped aside and waited for Mr. Lamotte to enter the way. "I believe most of you are acquainted with Mr. Lamotte."

Father glanced around the room and gave a decisive nod. "Well, we can now resolve all points of this matter, and nothing more will be said about it. It is bad enough that all our servants must be aware of it. Many of our neighbors must have a good idea what occurred last week."

Mama smoothed her gown. "My dear, leave our neighbors to me."

With a fond smile appearing on his face, Father moved to stand behind Mama's chair, and he rested his hand on her shoulder. When he focused again on Lamotte, who had not been invited to sit down, his face was severe. "If you would be so kind, tell everyone in this room what you told me yesterday evening, Mr. Lamotte."

Lamotte shifted from foot to foot. He focused his gaze on the wall. "I frequently amuse myself with card games as many gentlemen do," he said, his tone expressionless. "Mr. Miles Russell had the misfortune of losing to me earlier this year, and he handed over a family ring as security that he would repay the debt."

"And has the debt been repaid?" George asked.

Fidgeting, Lamotte cleared his throat. "It has not."

The answer made George shake his head reprovingly. Even though he had not been much a friend of late as one would have wished, I couldn't stand for Miles to be thought of disapprovingly. "As I recall, Mr. Russell attempted on several occasions to repay you, but you refused even to see him," I said. "Which, of course, begs the question: do you still have the ring, Mr. Lamotte?"

He glared at me before he said with reluctance, "I do not. When Oakcrest was broken into, the ring vanished. As you know, I suspected one of the servants, but the constable did not track down the culprit. Therefore, I dismissed them all and hoped I would find the item somewhere in the house."

Rosamund's cheeks flushed. "Can we get to the point?" she demanded. "I do have affairs to manage here in the house."

"Do you?" Mama asked, raising an eyebrow. "I had not realized that this was your house to manage, Rosamund."

The blush deepened on my sister-in-law's cheeks as George jumped to his wife's defense. "Mama, you know you have been unwell, and Rosamund has been of help to you." He took Rosamund's hand, only to have her to pull away from him.

Father huffed and shook his head. "The management of this household is not why we have gathered here," he said. He focused on Lamotte. "Would you be able to identify the ring were you to see it again, sir?"

"I would," Lamotte said, giving a brief nod. "I suspect it to be long gone, though. Sold to anyone who would offer a good price for it."

The drawing room door opened. "Mr. Ramsey and Mr. Russell," Butler announced before stepping aside.

"Oh," Mr. Ramsey said, taking in the group. "I had not realized we would be interrupting. We can return another time."

"No, you are exactly on time," Father said, gesturing for them both to come in. "We were just discussing a certain ring that Mr. Russell gave Mr. Lamotte as security for a debt. I don't suppose either of you have seen it? I would appreciate it if Mr. Lamotte would identify it so that we may bring this whole affair to an end."

Miles cleared his throat and reached for his pocket. "This ring, sir?" he asked, holding it out.

Raising an enquiring eyebrow, Father stared at Lamotte. The man stepped forward and picked up the ring from Miles' palm. "It is the ring," he said after studying it for a moment. He sent an accusing glare at Miles. "How did you get this, sir? Did you break into my house?"

"I did not!" Miles protested, bristling in anger at the accusation.

"Interesting," Father said, holding out his hand. He held the ring up to the light as if to examine it. The rest of us had become mere spectators to what was happening. "Rosamund, do you by any chance recognize the ring?"

How refreshing it was to sit and watch the deceptions unravel right before my eyes. Rosamund pursed her lips as she stared at the ring. For a moment, her face betrayed her struggle. If she identified it, how she acquired the ring would be called into question. "I do not recognize it," she finally said.

"And do you George?"

My brother was silent for several moments before he said, "I do not."

"Would you be able to identify the ring stolen from your wife?" Father next asked.

My brother shook his head. "I never pay much attention to Rosamund's baubles. One is much like the other in my opinion."

Rosamund scowled at him, but she said nothing. A refreshing change, in my opinion.

"Well, as far as I see it, we shall simply have to consign the unfortunate matter of the highwayman off as a thoughtless prank by a young person who was having a lark," Father said, taking charge of the situation. "Lucas was simply the unfortunate victim of being in the wrong place at the wrong time. There is no evidence that he is to blame or that he had any part of the affair. Rosamund, would you say your ring was truly worth a great deal? Should we pursue the matter?"

She raised her chin. "I would not. A worthless piece of jewelry. I cannot think why I even kept it."

Miles made a move to protest the description of the ring. "You're right, Mr. Russell," Father said. Whether he deliberately mistook my friend's action or not, I couldn't tell. "All that needs to be done is for you to repay Mr. Lamotte and count yourself lucky this matter has been resolved. Perhaps in the future, you will refrain from wasting your funds and time on cards."

With little grace, Miles acceded. "Mr. Lamotte, I will call upon you at your earliest convenience," he said.

Lamotte gave a sharp nod, his expression a mixture of relief and annoyance at the turn of events.

"And now, with this unsavory topic closed, we can move onto more pleasant matters," Father said, turning his attention to his old friend. "Did Phoebe not come with you? I would have thought she would be anxious to know that all was well with Lucas."

Mr. Ramsey cleared his throat. "I'm sorry to have to tell you this, Bywood, but I do wish this had been resolved earlier. Given everything that has happened, Phoebe has informed me she will not be connected in anyway to your son and that she wishes to accept young Mr. Russell's proposal."

All traces of easiness vanished from my father's face as he stared at his friend. Mama's smile was broad. "An excellent match," she said with enthusiasm. "We wish them much happiness together."

"Are you agreeable to this?" Mr. Ramsey asked, turning his gaze to me. "You know how changeable Phoebe is. If we wait a few days, she might—"

"Sir, I can tell you, nothing would bring me more joy," I interrupted swiftly. "May I offer my congratulations."

———— ◈ ————

"FOR ONE WHO HAS BEEN jilted, you seem remarkably at ease.

Glancing over my shoulder, I sent a grin at Ward, who was coming towards me. Phaeton took offense at my attention going elsewhere, and he nudged my shoulder. To appease the animal, I stroked my horse's nose. "I have been cleared of all wrongdoing," I said to the tall man as he came up beside me. "I find myself satisfied with that."

"Strange that Mrs. Bywood should suddenly decide the ring had no value after the fuss she made." Ward shook his head as he reached to pat Phaeton's neck. "I also heard a strange rumor that you were locked in your room to prevent you from fleeing the country."

"A true account, and not by my father's decree." The finer details, mainly an apology from George for confining me, had been set aside by my father's outrage. He'd had his heart set on my marriage to Phoebe, and I suspected it would take some time for him to reconcile himself to the matter. "Still, I am delighted to be free once again."

"And how long before you are off to purchase your cottage in Italy?"

"Sadly, my mother has requested me to reconsider my plans. I shall have to work out some other goal for my future."

Ward leaned against the fence, ignoring Phaeton's attempt to get his attention. "I'm sure you won't mind me saying this, but you ought to have more care in those you call friends and the schemes you allow yourself to be drawn into."

"Perhaps. But I don't think all of them are shabby fellows," I said, nodding in his direction. "I hear you defended me most vehemently and I thank you for it, Ward. When not many would have believed a word I said, you didn't even question whether I was innocent or not."

"I pride myself on being an excellent judge of character."

"Better than I, at any rate."

He dismissively raised a shoulder. "You are not the only one to have an acquaintance suddenly become someone you do not even recognize."

Shaking my head at the turn of conversation, I pushed away from the fence. My father and I had already discussed Miles' failings, and I had promised not to allow my friends to lead me into trouble again. Though Father had acknowledged, I'd been honorable in keeping my friend's confidence. It was a small step, perhaps, into my father and I becoming more amenable to each other.

"Will you be staying for Miss Ramsey and Mr. Russell's wedding?" I asked, pulling my thoughts to the present. "I was informed they are eager to get to the parson's mousetrap."

Miles and Phoebe had made little effort at circumspection since Mr. Ramsey had announced their betrothal. Phoebe's parents, out of fear she would break another engagement, were pressing for them to be married sooner rather than later. Thus, the house party, or what remained of it, would end with their wedding.

Ward fell into step beside me. "I expect so, though the house party has rather become less enjoyable than one might have hoped. Then, I shall take myself off to Bath."

"Bath? What takes you there?"

"You ask the most impertinent questions at times, Bywood."

With a laugh, I led the way to the gardens. "I do at that. It is no wonder that I am considered to be poor company."

Jane waved at us from where she sat next to Mama on the terrace. "I am told your brother and sister-in-law will be making their home in your father's small estate," Ward said. "That must be a relief to your whole family."

It was, but he had no right to say so. "One might say that is an impertinent observation."

One of Ward's rare grins appeared for the briefest moment. "Perhaps I could persuade you to accompany me to Bath. I've found it more enjoyable to go about with someone on whom I can rely."

His offer came as a surprise, but it was something I only considered for half a second. "I believe I've had enough of society."

"A little more time with your family and you will be begging to take me up on my offer," Ward said with a light laugh. He raised his eyebrow at me. "Unless there is something —or should I say, someone— keeping you here."

I refused to be led into confidences that would only be speculation. "Can I persuade you to join us for dinner, Ward? I know my mother has expressed a desire to be better acquainted with you."

"What tales have you been telling her?" he asked, and I thought he was about to refuse the invitation. "I would be delighted. Anything will be better than being forced to observe two love-sick fools falling over each other."

"Instead, you will be in the middle of a large family gathering where no doubt one of us will find some fault with another," I said to warn him. "It will be a loud affair and Rosamund will no doubt glare at us."

A strange expression crossed his face. "As I come from a small family, the experience of a large one will be welcome."

"Well, never say I didn't warn you."

"Did you ever discover the truth behind your mother's fall?" Ward asked, changing the subject.

I shook my head. "I have my suspicions. I cannot think it a coincidence that Lamotte should lose the ring, refuse to meet with Miles, and then a hole mysteriously appears in the shortcut between Bywood Hall and Oakcrest. It is a suspicion that I cannot prove, however, so I shall have to content myself with knowing Lamotte shall not be dwelling in the neighborhood."

Still, not knowing definitely was not satisfactory. Perhaps in the future I would find a definitive answer.

Our conversation was interrupted by Jane's two children, Julia, and Tristan, who came running towards us. Laughing, Ward caught Tristan up, causing loud squeals of joy. Unable to do the same to Julia, as my arm was still healing, I made do with chasing her around the bushes.

This was exactly my idea of a perfectly normal spring day.

Epilogue

Phoebe made a beautiful, blushing bride, though her joy was dampened by the rainstorm that hit the morning she became Miles' wife. Her initial wish had been that the entire Bywood family not attend. Her mother managed to convince her that such a slight was undeserved. Thus, with Jane and her husband still at Bywood Hall, there was a large number of Bywoods who witnessed her marriage.

The wedding breakfast was lively, with everyone in high spirits. Miles spent every moment by his bride's side, just as he had spent every waking moment with her during their short engagement.

A break in the rain meant that I could escape the noise and merriment for the gardens. I had only been there a few minutes when I realized I was not alone.

"I suppose you think you have made a narrow escape," Miss Darkin said as she walked to my side. She gave a smile, her blue eyes sparkling with delight. "For a short time, I believed Phoebe would marry you no matter what tale you spun or what mischief you caused."

"You and I both," I said with a laugh. "For a time there, I thought I would have to do something desperate and ill-advised. But all's well that end's well, though, and all that. May I escort you around the garden, Miss Darkin?"

She had been so occupied with helping Phoebe prepare for the wedding that I had hardly seen her at all since the foiled race between Ward and I. "I think not, sir," she said. "I cannot be away too long, otherwise gossiping tongues might begin to wag."

Disappointment hit and I fought not to allow it to show. "Of course. Perhaps I can walk in with you. No one could find fault with that, I am sure."

Miss Darkin sighed. "Mr. Bywood, please consider this from my point of view. No more than a month ago, you were practically betrothed to be married. Any kind of pursuit at this time would be improper. Surely you understand that."

As dismissals went, it was kind. "Forgive me," I said, offering a slight bow. "No offense was intended."

She tilted her head, and a smile played on her lips. "As I did not say it was unwelcome, I am not offended," she said. "My aunt and I stay on at Lamridge for the rest of the month. Perhaps, during our stay, you will show me some of those lovely vistas for painting that you mentioned?"

Startled, I blinked at her. Offering one last smile, she walked ahead of me. A laugh left my lips, and I rushed to catch up to her.

Lucas' story will continue in Best Laid Plans

Continue reading for a sneak peek!

Best Laid Plans

(A Gentleman of Misfortune, Book 2)

Chapter One

"Come on, old boy! You can do it! Come on!"

My words of encouragement blended with the sound of hooves hitting the ground. The wind whistled past my ears. Phaeton's sides heaved with exertion as he raced along the road. I leaned over his neck, urging him to go faster. To my right, Mr. John Ward was keeping pace beside me on his own mount, Tesoro.

Unless there was a sudden change, it looked as though it was going to be a tie between us. Again.

Since the first time we had attempted a race, Mr. Ward and I had tried three times to prove the superiority of our respective mount. Each time we had been evenly matched and nothing had been settled. In fact, I believed a few of the more intelligent of my family's tenants had earned themselves some coins with a wager that there would be another impasse.

Ahead of us, I could see the crossroad that marked the end of our race. There were fewer observers waiting there than there had been for the previous races. I suppose there was little excitement in observing a race where the two participants had already shown themselves evenly matched.

I brought Phaeton to a walk. Mr. Ward straightened up in his saddle as he did the same. "Well run, Bywood," he said.

"Same to you, Ward," I said with a nod. "I hope Geoffrey was watching closely. If I had to guess, it was close once again. Too close, I would wager, for any definite ruling."

He let out a laugh, which took me aback for a moment. There had been very few moments in our acquaintance when he appeared to actually enjoy himself. "If that is the case, I believe we shall simply have to accept the fact that Tesoro and Phaeton are too well matched for either of us to claim one or the other to be superior and cry quits on the matter."

We walked back to where Geoffrey, my family's faithful groom, was waiting. Before we had even reached him, the older man was shaking his head. "I'm sorry Mr. Lucas," he called out. "You both crossed the line at the same moment from my point of view."

Though I had expected as much, I couldn't hold back a sigh. "Well, that's that then,"

"You're not going to try again?" There was a hopeful note in the groom's voice that made me grin.

"Ward and I agree it's probably for the best. We'll just have to find some other boasting gentleman to defeat."

"We're not going to have much success around here," Ward said, waving his had vaguely at the countryside. "I do believe most every one of your neighbors has at least heard about our friendly competition. I doubt any of them are willing to challenge either of us."

He was absolutely right, but I wasn't worried about the matter. Most everyone in the neighborhood knew of the Bywood penchant for excellent mounts. Only visitors had ever dared challenge us, and it was rare that any of them found victory.

I glanced around and saw everyone drifting to return to their daily tasks. Geoffrey mounted his own horse and headed back to Bywood Hall.

"What plans have you for the rest of the day, Ward?" I asked, turning my attention to the next possible amusement. "Would you care for a bit of fishing?"

My friend shook his head. "Not today, Bywood. I have business correspondence that requires my attention, a task I have been putting aside for far too long. Perhaps another day."

He didn't wait for me to voice an acknowledgment before he wheeled Tesoro around and set off. Of course he would have business to see to. It seemed everyone had something to see to, and I did not.

The investment of my inheritance was sound and did not require my attention at every change. I did not yet have an estate to oversee, and no wife to attend, so there was little to occupy my time.

Resisting the urge to sigh, I nudged Phaeton into a trot. Perhaps my sister's children would provide some entertainment.

◆◆◆

"Once upon a time, there was a young man of modest fortune, who was so hounded by his family that he despaired of ever satisfying them all. Giving up on ever succeeding, he died and all who knew him lamented the loss of a good fellow. The end."

One on either side of me, my niece and nephew giggled at my dramatic words. Out of the corner of my eye, I saw my sister, Jane Castleton, shake her head. "Good heavens, Lucas Bywood!" she said, her tone reproving. "What kind of a story is that to be telling my children? No one ever died because his family gave him advice."

"You hear that?" I said to the young ones who were listening with great interest. "Your mama knows best about everything. You must never disagree or argue with her."

"Luke, I'm close to losing my patience with you."

Never let it be said I didn't know when I had pushed my luck too far. "Why don't you two go find your Aunt Philippa and discover if she's still visiting with Mr. Gaylord," I said to the two children. "I think they would be delighted to see you."

"What? No!" Jane exclaimed as Julia and Tristan took off running. "Lucas! How could you? Philly needs time with her betrothed. It's cruel to send my children to pester them. How would you feel if we did the same thing when you wished to have a private conversation with Miss Darkin?"

Thoughts of Miss Olivia Darkin's smiling face and sparkling eyes crossed my mind. "I can't think of any time when I wouldn't be happy to see my nephew and niece," I said, mentally pushing aside the memories. "Besides, Miss Darkin isn't here for there to be a situation such as you describe. Also, you forget I am not betrothed to her, so such an intimate setting would be a scandal. I am astonished you would even suggest such a thing, Jane."

"Why haven't you asked her to marry you?" Jane asked, crossing the room to be by my side. She put her hand on my shoulder, and her tone became wheedling. "You've had plenty of time to know her. She's a lovely girl, and after everything that has happened—"

"You're hounding me again, Jane."

"This isn't hounding. I just want to know what you're thinking," Jane said, her tone frustrated. "I thought you liked Miss Darkin, and it's quite understandable why you would.

She's a lovely young woman and I believe she will make you a perfect life companion. Why haven't—"

"I can hear the gossip now," I said, unashamed to interrupt her. I raised my voice to a falsetto. "'Poor young Mr. Bywood. Who would have guessed he would die from his family constantly giving him advice and questioning him? Have you ever heard the like?'"

Throwing up her hands, Jane turned away. "I am done trying to talk sense into you. You are determined to be difficult."

"Jane, Miss Darkin asked for me to wait for a time before pursuing her," I said impulsively. I disliked disappointing my oldest sister and I hoped she would understand. "She is a friend of Phoebe, and did not feel it would be appropriate for us to pursue a courtship in view of everything that happened in the last month."

"I've never heard anything more ridiculous! You made it clear you had no attachment to Phoebe Ramsey, whatever Father may have said on the matter. No one would have thought bad of you if you chose instead to pursue Miss Darkin, especially as Phoebe is now Mrs. Russell."

"And what kind of gentleman would I have been to ignore a lady's wishes?" I asked, offended by the idea.

"Well, I'm sure she had no idea that she would be summoned back home to assist in the care of her sick siblings," Jane said, sending a glare at me over her shoulder. "You will lose your chance if you do not follow her."

I couldn't help but laugh at her words. "Follow her straight into a situation where I would be unable to see her due to her responsibility to care for her siblings? Hardly the right time to woo a lady, Jane. Really, your idea of helpful suggestions is dreadfully skewed."

"Faint heart never won fair lady."

"Neither have foolish actions."

It had only been a few days since Miss Darkin had left the neighboring estate. In that time, it seemed as though everyone in the family had inquired after my intentions toward the lady. Did I plan to continue the acquaintance? Was there a private agreement between us? Wasn't she a lovely girl?

When compared to the ill opinion most had given voice to earlier in the summer, these questions and urgings not to allow Miss Darkin to escape were easier to hear. However, it hadn't taken long for such questioning to become exceedingly tiresome, especially as I considered it a personal matter. Why such interest in whop I would wed? It wasn't as if I were the heir.

I was fond of Miss Darkin, it was true. She was sensible, without any trace of the silliness I had seen in many other young ladies of my generation. Her sense of humor was similar to my own and most of the time we had been together had been spent in laughter. Even a fool could see we were well-matched, perhaps better than some married couples.

While I had been disappointed with her request to wait, I could acknowledge the wisdom behind it. I'd been 'courting' Phoebe Ramsey, now Mrs. Miles Russell, for several weeks and gossip would always result if I were, in the eyes of the neighborhood biddies, to pursue another lady so soon after Phoebe and Miles' wedding.

Thinking of my friend and his new wife, I wondered how they were getting on. They had gone somewhere south for their wedding trip, and I knew they were expected to return to her parents' home in a few weeks. With only each other for company, did they still regard each other with the same fondness? Or would the first flush of love have left them?

I intended to be as far from the neighborhood as I could reasonably manage to be when they returned.

"There are times I would dearly like to box your ears. Maybe that would knock some sense into you."

Jane's frustrated voice pulled me from my thoughts. "You've done so in the past. What's keeping you from doing so now?" I asked curiously.

"You are taller than I, and I fear you would find some way to retaliate," Jane said, a smile pulling at the corners of her mouth though she tried to hide it with a stern expression. "Luke, be serious for a moment. Do you not want to be settled? Have your own family? A loving wife and children?"

"At two and twenty, I have plenty of time to settle down. I thought you were on my side, Jane! Did you not say it was good for me to take a Grand Tour and travel to see something of the world?"

"Yes, I did. However, the one does not have anything to do with the other. You've traveled, seen the world, and now you are back home. It is time for you to turn your attention to other matters."

"Well, if that is the case, I shall simply have to continue my travels. After all, I never did make it to Paris."

My sister's eyes widened. "Lucas! That is not what I was suggesting! After everything that has happened, how could you possibly believe France a good place to visit?"

"Jane! Jane!" Phillipa's voice reached us both. Our youngest sister's tone was definitely one of annoyance. "You must do something with your children!"

As a distraction, it was excellent. "I told you not to send them after her! One moment, Philly." Jane hurried to rescue Phillipa, leaving me to make my own escape.

Acknowledgments

This book would not be what it is today without the help of a few other people. A huge thank you to Brianna McClure for editing and polishing. Davette Pitman caught many little mistakes and is an amazing beta reader. Thank you to my sister for being my first reader, and my mom for being my first critic. I'm thankful to my writer's group for always supporting me. And, of course, I can't forget about my lovely followers on Wattpad for being with me from the beginning.

You all rock!

Also Available By Bethany Swafford

T he Sinclair Society Series:
   Regency Rumors
   Eugenia (A Sinclair Society Novella)
   The Debutante
   Grace (A Sinclair Society Novella)
   Clarendon Estate
   The Cousins
   Emily's Choice
   Lady Evan Wins the Day
   Standalone Novels:
   A Chaotic Courtship
   My Hands Hold My Story

About the Author

For as long as she can remember, Bethany Swafford has loved reading books. That love of words extended to writing as she grew older and when it became more difficult to find a 'clean' book, she determined to write her own. Among her favorite authors are Jane Austen, Sir Arthur Conan Doyle, and Georgette Heyer. When she doesn't have a pen to paper (or fingertips to a laptop keyboard), she can be found with a book in hand.

To get notified about new releases and any news, sign up to Bethany's Newsletter here: https://bit.ly/2Hg7KJw

Read   more   at https://bethanyswaffordauthor.wordpress.com/.

Printed in the USA
CPSIA information can be obtained
at www.ICGtesting.com
LVHW090822070724
784826LV00033B/763

9 798885 268417